FINN'S FORTUNE

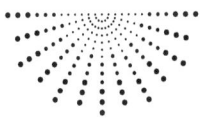

KATHLEEN BALL

Copyright © 2018 by Kathleen Ball

All rights reserved.

No part of this book may be reproduced in any form or by any electronic or mechanical means, including information storage and retrieval systems, without written permission from the author, except for the use of brief quotations in a book review.

❦ Created with Vellum

This one is for you Mo!
I got a lot of the inspiration for this novel from the life of my Grandfather, Thomas Tighe. He like the hero in this book had to leave Ireland and come to America to start a new life. He was an amazing man.

And to Bruce, Steven, Colt, Clara, and Emmy because I love them.

PREFACE

Langley's Legacy

"Beare and Forebeare" (be patient and endure)

Meet the Langley's who've traveled from their homeland of Ireland with only what they could carry. Along with the meager possessions brought from their homeland of Ireland, were a piece of lace and a silver pocket watch with the family motto "Beare and Forebeare" inscribed inside.

When the Langley's settled in New Dawn Springs, Oregon, little did they suspect the land would be a legacy to those who would come after them and that the land would be owned by the family for generations to come.

Follow the Langley's rich family history through the years as told through the wonderful storytelling voices of these six bestselling authors.

1850 - Finn's Fortune - Kathleen Ball
1875 - Patrick's Proposal - Hildie McQueen
1899 - Donovan's Deceit - Kathy Shaw
1933 - Aiden's Arrangement - Peggy McKenzie
1968 - Heath's Homecoming - Merry Farmer
Present - Collin's Challenge - Sylvia McDaniel

CHAPTER ONE

Maureen shivered and her teeth chattered while she struggled out of her improvised bed and put on her shawl. She shook her head. Everything was improvised but someday she'd have a grand house with a farm to match. All she needed to do was to figure out how to survive the frigid winter and then start planting.

The days were getting shorter, and she needed to work every hour of daylight. After grabbing some kindling and shavings, she climbed outside to build a fire. Abruptly, she stopped and stared. A wagon sat directly across the stream from her.

Her stomach tied into knots and a myriad of thoughts ran through her mind. She needed to concentrate on one thing: survival. As fast as lightning, she scrambled back into her wagon and got dressed. Then she pulled herself together, laid her fire and got her coffee boiling, glancing over her shoulder the whole time. She had a couple of firearms but wasn't exactly sure how they worked. Oh, she'd seen people use them plenty of times but she never had to load one herself.

She stilled when she saw movement in the other wagon. Her mouth dropped open when a brawny man with thick brown hair and blue eyes jumped to the ground. He wore only his pants, and the muscles in his chest flexed as he yawned and stretched his arms over his head. He froze in place as his gaze met hers.

Quickly, she averted her gaze to the ground lest he think she was ogling his indecency.

"Top of the mornin' to ya," he greeted in a strong Irish brogue. He nodded his head at her.

"Good morning. Will you be on your way soon?" She stood straight and tall not wanting him to think her a weak female.

"No. I do believe my traveling days are over. I'm putting down roots right here. I got my 320 acres at the claim office in New Dawn Springs yesterday." Though he mentioned the nearest town, he spread his arms and gestured to the land surrounding him. "I stocked up there as well, and here I am. Does your 320 acres start at the stream?"

"The stream is the boundary line. My husband and I were told we'd have to share it with whoever bought the property next to our 640 acres." She gave him a sweet smile. She hated it, but she'd have to lie again.

"Ah, so you're married. I'm Finn Langley recently from County Mayo, Ireland. Is your husband still sleeping?"

"I'm Maureen Mc— I mean Maureen Cleary." She forced a chuckle. "I'm recently married, so I'm still getting used to my married name. My husband Malcolm is at the far end of our property. We've had problems with squatters. I'm sure you'll meet him sometime." Dang, how was she supposed to find someone else to pretend to be her husband?

Finn ran his fingers through his brown hair, the motion setting off red highlights to sparkle in the early morning sunlight. "I'd like to meet him. Maybe we can help each other build our cabins."

Maureen crossed her arms in front of her. "From what I've heard, the stream floods on your side. You might want to build elsewhere on the property." She was sure to go to hell for her lies.

"Thanks for the warning." He grinned, and her stomach fluttered. "I'll take my chances." He gave her a knowing look.

Dang, he was on to her.

"How long have you and your husband been here?"

She shrugged. "About a month, I think. Why?"

"No reason. You haven't built much in the way of a cabin. I just wondered is all. It's not my business. I need to get dressed. I didn't realize my neighbor was female. I'll take care to be clothed in your presence from now on. What part of the old country are you from?"

"County Tyrone. I miss it," she added, fighting a wave of sadness She missed her family every day. "It was hard to say good-bye to my ma, but food was scarce and she had my brothers. I was another mouth to feed."

Finn nodded. "I left for reasons like that. How long have you been in America?"

She clasped her hands together. "Over five years now."

"Good on you. Have a good day." He climbed back into his wagon.

Maureen sat on a big rock near the fire and prayed for her soul. Almost everything she'd told Finn had been a lie. Except for where she was from and why she left. He was a fellow Irishman. Perhaps he could be trusted? Her throat tightened. No, she wouldn't put her fate in another's hands ever again.

She drank her coffee and then climbed into her wagon. Next, she hung out men's clothing on the wash line. Maybe this would fool him. As she studied the two shirts and the pair of worn trousers fluttering in the wind, her shoulders sagged. She'd need more than a few clothes to keep the charade up.

FINN SMILED. The view from his place was lovely indeed. The lass was a beauty. Her red hair and bright blue eyes had him longing for home. The home he had been forced to leave. He'd never see Ireland again. He sighed and took out the only thing he had left of his family. An ancient pocket watch. It had been handed down through the years to the eldest male Langley and inside was etched the family motto: *Beare and Forebeare*. The words meant be patient and endure. He shook his head. It really described much of his life so far. The outside of the silver watch had a shamrock etched on it, and he rubbed his finger over the design. It was probably worth some money, but it meant more to him than money. He chuckled. He hoped to still have it to hand down someday.

His first chore was to make sure his horse, Justice, was taken care of then he was off to fell some trees. He needed a cabin. He'd heard the winters could be nasty. He frowned. Maybe this Malcolm fellow wasn't familiar with cold weather. He was looking forward to meeting him.

When he was ready, he grabbed his gloves and axe. He looked but saw no sign of Mrs. Cleary or anyone who might be her husband. They probably had their own routine. He didn't have far to go to find fine, thick trees for his cabin. He'd be clearing some of the land for his horses. For the cattle, it didn't matter as much.

He chopped and chopped all day until he had several trees down. He kept glancing at the other wagon but he didn't see anyone about. It sure would be easier with two men, but he wouldn't have the option it seemed.

He stopped for the day and filled a bucket with cool water. Using a dipper, he drank his fill and then tended to his horse again. He started his fire and heated canned beans. Still there was no sign of the Clearys except the clothes that were hung to dry had been taken off the clothesline. From the size of the shirts he'd seen, Malcolm must be a bear of a man.

They weren't his business, but he wouldn't mind looking at the pretty lass again. He stared into the fire as it got darker and colder. He missed his ma the most. She'd cried when he left but he hadn't had a choice. There was a price on his head, and he'd had to get out of Ireland. He was a Fenian – the group of people in Ireland who wanted the English out of their country.

His job had been to recruit members and to find guns. He'd found plenty of guns in England and smuggled them into Ireland until he was caught. The treatment inside the prison was harsh and extremely hard to endure, but he and the lads had endured it and they'd survived. Well over a year ago, they'd broken out of prison. Finn went a different way than the rest and he was one of the few who hadn't been caught and shot. He'd had but a moment to say good-bye to his ma, and then he'd had help getting onto a ship bound for America.

Once he reached New York City, he had been greeted and treated very well by those brothers in arms who had also left Ireland for the same reason. But one day Tommy O'Dell came running and told him a traitor had turned Finn in for the money. Finn skedaddled to Independence Missouri and joined a wagon train to Oregon. He'd told no one where he was going. It was safer that way.

He'd built plenty of cabins in Ireland but they all had thatched roofs. He'd studied the cabins here as they rode by and he was confident he'd have no trouble building one.

Hopefully, Malcolm Cleary would end up a friend. It had been lonely traveling the trail, keeping to himself.

MAUREEN PILED every quilt she had on top of her. She didn't dare make a fire that night. Finn had too many questions. If he wasn't going to move, she'd have to. The thought of hauling water everyday didn't appeal to her but the thought of losing her land was unbearable. Maybe she could watch Finn and copy what he did to make herself a cabin. She'd just have to make excuses as to why Malcolm was never home. Having a plan, she felt better, and finally she fell asleep.

She awoke to the sound of chopping wood. Her serenity was gone. She quickly got dressed, put on the coffee, and grabbed a biscuit she'd made three days ago. Then she put some of her precious beans in water to soak. She'd be able to cook them tonight.

Catching sight of Finn made her heart beat faster. His shirt tightened against his corded back muscles when he moved. He seemed to be a good honest man, and if he knew of her lies he'd probably feel honor bound to turn her in.

She rubbed her hand over her eyes, feeling a bit weary before she even started. But she decided to buck up. Work always came first. She found her gloves and axe and set out to cut down a few trees. Finn had cut so many yesterday, and today he was having Justice pull them closer to his wagon. She'd sold her oxen for food and a mule named Contrary. She probably should have gotten a horse.

A smile graced her face. Contrary wouldn't pull logs. Maureen would have to try but she already knew she'd be the loser. But one thing at a time.

She stopped at the nearest tree and swung the axe. Frowning, she stared at the spot she had just hit. It looked as though it was barely scratched. Anything worth having was worth working for. She swung again and again and finally she saw under the bark.

Muscle strength wasn't her best attribute, but if she kept working, she'd get stronger every day. She had plenty of strength to build a farm. She'd get this done too.

After a long time, one tree fell. A bubble of delighted laughter started in her chest until she was laughing loud and clear. She didn't need a husband. If the snow held off long enough, she'd have her cabin built. A sense of accomplishment settled upon her. She glanced in Finn's direction and saw him scowl. What was his problem?

From his determined footsteps in her direction, she was bound to know in a minute.

"Good day, Mr. Langley."

"Yes it is. I, um… Why are you cutting trees close to where the house will be?"

She furrowed her brow. "Why not?"

"Trees will keep a cabin cooler in the summer and block some of the snow in the winter. I'd go out a bit and cut down ones in places where you plan to plant. You'll need to clear that area eventually won't you?"

She shrugged. "Malcolm must have told me and I forgot. Thank you, Mr. Langley for your wise counsel."

"Where is your husband, Mrs. Cleary? I'd sure like to meet him. I was thinking with two of us we could get both cabins up before winter. Many hands make light work as they say." He grinned at her until dimples appeared in both of his cheeks.

Oh, he was a handsome one, and he seemed to know it. There was no way she'd fall for a conceited Irishman. She'd met them all before, and she wasn't interested. They all seemed to gravitate toward her because of her red hair. But she knew better. She didn't need a man to make her farm successful.

"You must have just missed him. Malcolm went hunting." Another lie; she was going to hell for sure.

"Tell you what. We could share the hunting duty and share the meat we get."

She frowned at him and his eyes widened.

"I'm sorry for being too forward, Mrs. Cleary. I was just hoping neighbor could help neighbor. I can see the idea isn't to your liking." He studied her for a moment. "I have a lot of work to do. Some of the men in town talked about an early winter, and I want to be ready. Good day, Mrs. Cleary."

She watched him walk away. He had quite the swagger. She picked up her axe and headed out away from where the house would be. The muscles in her arms, shoulders and back all burned but she had to go on. It took the rest of the day to fell another tree.

It took all her energy to walk back to her wagon. Thankfully, all she had to do was put the beans over the fire. She added wood shavings to the banked fire and quick enough a flame burned. Glancing over at Finn's camp, she saw him eating beans out of a can.

If only she had the nerve to invite him to share her supper. He was right about neighbor helping neighbor. That was how they'd all survived in Ireland. She'd have to kill off Malcolm. It would be a lot of trouble. From what she'd read, if a husband died, the widow got all the land.

How should he die? It would have to be something that wouldn't involve questions or a doctor. She'd head out with her shovel tomorrow and dig a grave and then refill it. A makeshift cross would be his grave marker.

No one had met her fake husband, so she didn't expect much sympathy. She didn't need to go to New Dawn Springs in the near future anyway. When she was done, she'd mention it to Finn and that would stop all the questions about her husband. She sighed loudly. One lie was leading to another, and that was not how she wanted to live her life.

The beans were pretty good, and she'd made enough to last a few days. After she was done, she banked her fire and went to bed. She had a big day tomorrow. She still had to figure out how her husband had died.

WHERE COULD SHE BE? Finn kept looking for her, but she'd been gone all day. At least she'd taken that mule of hers. He chopped down another tree. Did she at least have a gun? The sun was beginning to set, and he worried even more.

He sat next to his fire and reminded himself that she had a husband. She was probably snuggling up to him right now. He ran his fingers through his hair. She was not of his concern. He had enough of his own problems to deal with.

Staring into the fire, he stayed up much later than usual, hoping to catch a glimpse of Maureen. Finally, admitting to himself she wouldn't be back, he stood and stretched. Movement in the distance caught his attention. He looked again and didn't see anything. After rubbing his eyes, he peered again and there was someone walking slowly with a mule. He furrowed his brow. Maureen Cleary. Where was her husband? Finn shrugged. Probably doing whatever it was he had been doing before.

He almost decided to go into his wagon, but the way she limped stopped him. He didn't know enough about the terrain to guess where she'd been. Her body looked weary, and her movements were slow. He ran in her direction and caught her as she fell. Her dress was heavy with mud and it made carrying her difficult. Even her mule was caked in the stuff.

Letting go of the mule's lead, she hung her head. "Malcolm is dead."

"Malcolm your husband?" She nodded. "What happened? Where is he?"

"I buried him in the forest. He's a big man and the hole took forever to dig. There was so much mud. I don't understand it. It's dry here."

"It might have rained where you buried him."

She nodded absently.

"How did he die?"

She stared out to the horizon. "His horse must have thrown him. His head lay on a rock with blood on it. I looked but I didn't see the bay anywhere."

He tightened his arms around her to comfort her. "How long had you been married?"

"Not long. We met on a wagon train coming to Oregon. I don't even know who to notify. He said he was alone in the world."

Finn turned her toward the direction of his fire. "Come let's get you warm while I take care of your mule." He seated her on a wooden crate and handed her a cup of coffee. Then he took the mule and led her to the stream. He'd brought a bucket and brush with him and gave her a bath. She brayed and brayed, but finally she was clean.

He glanced at Maureen and she looked to be breathing even again. Sitting next to her, he took her hand in his. "I'm so sorry for your loss, lass."

She nodded. "Thank you. It's bad timing but I'll be able to get along just fine."

Bad timing? Perhaps hers wasn't a love match. Many married for convenience. It was a lot of work to make a home, and two were better than one. She wasn't his problem, he reminded himself. He tended to be too helpful and often left himself without. Not this time. This time he was going to make his fortune right here in Oregon. The soil was rich, there seemed to be mavericks aplenty to make a decent herd, and he had Justice to sire any mares he caught. He had more here than he'd ever had and the possibilities were endless.

"Was there any sign of the squatters? It's strange that people would squat when there was free land to be had." She stiffened.

"That's what Malcolm said. Now hearing it from you, it doesn't make much sense does it? He wasn't one to lie."

"I didn't say he lied, I'm just curious is all. You dug the grave yourself and buried him? No wonder you look worn to the bone. We need to get this dress off you. It's mud caked and heavy as all get out."

She simply nodded. His heart ached for her loss. What was she going to do out here alone? He sighed. It wasn't his problem.

It became his problem as soon as he got her to her wagon. She needed help getting the weighted dress off and he had to close his eyes to help. He'd grown up in a big Irish Catholic family and he'd plenty of sisters. It certainly wouldn't be the first time he'd seen a female in a shift.

He unbuttoned and helped her get out of the contraption she called a dress. He did have to open his eyes at one point and he gulped. Maureen was no comparison to his sisters. She was a real woman, and the sight of her made his blood run hot. He went and got her some heated water from his fire and gave it to her along with a clean cloth.

"Let me know if you need anything. Do you want me to search for the horse in the morning?"

"He'll come home eventually. Most horses do." Her voice was so weary he decided to drop the subject.

He waited until she was finished and in her nightclothes. "Let's get you some food."

She began to climb out of the wagon when he scooped

her up and carried her to his fire. "I think I'll have to make a better bridge for us to cross. Three logs tied together isn't the best."

"It was here when we got here. We came in from the other direction so we had no need to cross it," she said in a low voice.

He put her down on a crate and then handed her a plate of food.

She gave him a faint smile. "You got yourself a deer after all."

"Venison is my favorite. There's plenty for the both of us."

Her gaze flew to his face and she shook her head. "I can make it on my own. I'm not your worry."

Finn didn't answer her. She had no idea what it took to make it out here with winter biting at their heels. If her husband had any smarts he would have started a cabin on the first day. Not his worry? Who was she trying to convince? Him or herself? He'd have to watch her freeze to death all winter. She probably didn't have enough provisions either. He wished he could give her a reassuring smile, but he just couldn't. For all he knew she was a shrew, a pretty one but a shrew just the same.

He couldn't afford to have anyone getting close to him. He might have to run at a moment's notice. He'd been too proud to change his last name from Langley and he hoped he wouldn't have reason to regret it. The Langley name was known for honesty, generosity, and fierce fighting against the British. He inwardly groaned. He'd have to work twice as hard and get two structures up by winter.

He frowned. That wouldn't work either. It would be near impossible to make two cabins before the first snow. She needed to go back to town. Surely, she'd made some friends on her long trek to Oregon. One of them would take her in.

Men would be lining up to get a hold of her property. It was one of the better ones.

He gazed back at her. Would she take the first offer? He didn't fancy beating a man to pulp if he laid a wrong hand on her. "I'll take you to town tomorrow so you can make arrangements."

Her jaw dropped and her brow furrowed. "Arrangements?"

"Yes. You can find someone to stay with. It's not safe for you on your own. I wish I had the time to help you, but I barely have time to get a cabin up for myself."

Her eyes flashed with anger as she stood up. She put one hand on her hip. "I told you I can make it on my own, and I plan to do just that. I don't need to make other arrangements." She shoved her plate at him then stormed off across the bridge and climbed into her wagon.

He sighed. Of all the women in the world, why had he ended up next to the most stubborn of them all? He'd give her time to grieve and come to her senses before he insisted on taking her back to town. By then she'd be practically begging him to get her to a safe place for the winter.

CHAPTER TWO

Though the days were getting crisp, sweat formed on her forehead, and she had to stop to wipe it away. Dragging logs was hard work, but she only had this last one to deal with. Every day she spied on Finn to see what he was doing, and she did the same. Not at the same pace, but she memorized what needed to be done.

He had his walls almost built up and she'd yet to start but she had enough logs. She wasn't as tall as Finn was so she decided to make her cabin shorter. He'd offered to help once, but she turned him down. Now he only offered to take her back to town.

No matter how hard she had to work, she was going to be free. If a person thought they owned another, they tried to take every advantage and a woman could hardly say no. She'd run before she'd been disgraced, but looking over her shoulder wasn't complete freedom.

She felt a moment of triumph when she put the last log with the others. Taking a deep breath, she smiled. Next was to lay out the cabin. She dragged the logs into a small square shape and then took a step back to admire her work.

"Looks good!" A man's voice boomed.

She spun around and was alarmed to see a rather big man on a chestnut horse riding in her direction.

"The name is Cleary. John Cleary, your brother-in-law. I'm looking for Malcolm. Surprised I was, to learn of his marriage. Looks like he picked out a nice piece of land."

She furrowed her brow. What was this man playing at? There wasn't a Malcolm. Somehow, this man knew it. She studied him a bit. Now what?

John dismounted and smiled at her. "Where is that brother of mine?"

"I think you've made a mistake. My Malcolm didn't have any relations."

"In America. He has plenty in Ireland. I got here as fast as I could when I found I'd just missed him. We always planned to build a horse ranch together."

"See, there you go. My Malcolm was a farmer."

John frowned and took a step toward her. "Was?"

"Yes, I'm sorry to say he died about ten days ago."

He growled. "You didn't report his death to the authorities?"

Maureen took a step back. "I haven't been able to get to town. I have a cabin to build."

"On my land." He glared at her.

"Oh no, you're mistaken. This is my land, and it's all legal."

He took two long strides and put his hand around the front of her throat. "It's what I say it is. In fact I think poor Malcom would have wanted me to marry you and keep you safe."

She gasped for air before he pushed her to the ground and shook his head at her in disgust.

"What did you say your name was?" His eyes narrowed.

"Maureen Cleary." She sat up rubbing her bruised throat. She started to stand but he pushed her again.

"Where is all the money?" His voice seemed to grow louder with each question.

"There is no money. We planned to work hard to get the farm going. I really think you have the wrong Malcolm Cleary."

"Shut your mouth! I don't ever want to know what you think. Now, I'm hungry and I expect you to make me something to eat."

Her mouth fell open and she stared.

"Now!" he barked

Fear coursed through her body. Why hadn't she learned how to use a gun? She glanced over at Finn's place, but he wasn't there. Who was this man? Either he had the wrong Cleary or he was trying to swindle her property from her. It must be the wrong Cleary. It didn't matter, he needed to leave.

Her whole body shook as she stood, half waiting for him to knock her down again. She had biscuits to offer but that probably wasn't what he had in mind. She started the task of getting the fire going and making a stew using meat in a jar she'd purchased from the general store. She threw in small pieces of potatoes and hoped it wouldn't take too long to cook.

She didn't like the gleam in John's eyes. She should have said Malcolm would be back. There was no help for it now. She wiped her hands on a cloth and walked toward her logs. She dragged few more into place while John stared at her.

"Did you want to help me out, dear brother-in-law? I bet Malcolm would have wanted you to build my cabin for me. In fact, he would have expected no less from a family member." She bit the inside of her lip to keep from smiling.

For someone supposedly right off the boat, John didn't have a heavy brogue.

He didn't acknowledge her.

"How is your Aunt Bess getting on? Malcolm was worried about her."

"Fine, she's just fine," he answered sounding agitated.

Now she had her answer. He never knew the fictitious Malcolm and the make believe Aunt Bess. Somehow, he knew something, though. So far, he hadn't accused her of having a fake husband. Relief swept through her at the sound of Finn arriving on Justice.

He swung down and caught her eye, giving her slight nod as though to let her know he understood she was in distress. "Hello there! I'm Finn Langley, and you are?"

"John Cleary here. I came to live with my brother, but I hear he's dead. I'm trying to persuade the little widow here it's *MY* duty to marry her now."

Finn glanced at her before he sat down across from John. "Where do you hail from, John?"

John's lips were pressed into a straight line. "County Mayo, you?"

"The very same." He angled his head and studied the newcomer. "I know most of the Clearys there, and I can't place you. Which is your family?"

John shifted on the crate he sat on. "There are so many of us, I even have a hard time keeping up with the family." He gave them a fake laugh.

"Surely you know Shamus and his wife Maeve. They're the head of the clan it seemed to me." Finn smiled conversationally. Maureen was impressed.

"Did I say Mayo? I don't know what I was thinking. I'm from Cork."

Finn nodded. "I know the Cork Cleary's too. My ma's sister married a Cork Cleary. Nice folks all of them."

John shook his head and sneered at Finn. "You sure do get around. You must be part of the Fenian scum." He practically spat at Finn.

Finn pulled a gun. "Give it up. You're from the north. I bet you're protestant too."

John laughed. "I recognize the name now. Finnegan Langley. There's a price on your head." John pulled out his gun and shot in Finn's direction.

Maureen screamed at the gunfire and it was over in a flash. John was dead. She swayed a bit but held on to her wagon wheel. She stared at Finn and he stared back.

"There is no husband is there?"

She just shook her head.

Finn grabbed an oilcloth and wrapped John in it and then lifted him onto the chestnut. "Put a coat on, we'll need to ride to where you buried your 'husband.'" He grabbed some gear and tied it up on Justice.

She could hardly catch her breath. There was a grave but it was empty. "Finn, no one is buried in the grave."

He shot her a look of annoyance. "I just figured that one out. Let's go."

She walked toward Contrary and Finn laughed. "She'll take you in circles. Come on and ride with me. You can fill me in on the lurid details as we ride."

She was very careful and gave him only the particulars he needed to know and nothing more. She needed to protect herself. She prayed that her past never came knocking on her door.

FINN WAS STILL REELING from what had just happened at the campfire. No husband? She'd got that one past him easily enough. John wasn't as lucky. He'd planned to have both

Maureen and the land for himself. Somehow, he'd found out she was alone but how? People probably spied on the ones with the better lots of land. Maybe he just wanted Maureen for himself. Now Finn was exposed, just to Maureen but exposed nonetheless. He'd have to think on it.

It was a bit of a ride to the grave, and the feel of Maureen leaning back against him as they rode awakened something within him that he hadn't felt for a very long time. It wasn't just her sweet body; it was all of her. He needed to be careful, or he'd be hogtied to her before he knew it.

"Why is your neck so red?"

She shook her head.

"Did that brute touch you?"

"You're squeezing me."

He loosened his hold on her. "I'm sorry. What happened to your neck?"

"He wanted to show me he was the boss and that I was to do whatever he wanted."

Finn stiffened. "He didn't—"

"No, he didn't get a chance. You came just in time. How did he know about Malcolm?"

"I don't know, lass. We'll need to be more aware of our surroundings to see who is watching us."

She nodded. "Stop. The grave is right there."

It looked like a fresh grave all right. He got down then lifted his arms up to help Maureen down. She slid easily into his arms. He laughed. "I hadn't realized just how wee you are."

"It's you who is abnormally tall." She smiled back at him. Then, her smile faded. "We have a body to bury."

His smile died too. "Yes, lass we do."

Her hand covered her mouth for a second. "What if he has friends? What if they know where he went? What if they come looking for him?" Her breathing became ragged.

He put a hand on her shoulder. "One thing at a time. We can't control anything but burying him right now. No one followed us. I checked as we rode."

She shot him a grim look. "You're right, one thing at a time."

Finn grabbed the shovel and began to dig. At least the soil was still loose and it made for easier digging. He paused and took a drink from the tin canteen Maureen handed him. "You certainly dug deep. This grave is huge!"

"Malcolm was supposed to be a big man. I was afraid you'd want to see the grave. I was in a panic. I really never thought I'd have a neighbor so close to me. I never considered I'd have to produce Malcolm to anyone." She took the canteen back and seemed to look everywhere except at him.

He wanted to question her but it wasn't the time or place. She must have had her reasons. Maybe she was just greedy and wanted 640 acres due a married couple. In reality, he knew nothing about her. She'd be wanting answers too, he supposed. Could he trust her? If she spilled her secret, he'd spill his—maybe.

He pulled the body off the horse and opened the oilcloth. He checked the man's pockets and came up with a measly amount of money. But there wasn't a clue as to who he really was. Maureen helped him to pull John to the grave and they rolled him into it. Finn made quick work covering the body.

Next, he checked the saddlebags and came up empty. He slapped the horse on its hind flank and sent him off. "Nice horse."

"Yes indeed. Too bad we had to chase him away, but we don't want anyone to know John was ever here." Maureen put the makeshift cross she'd made for Malcolm at the head of the grave. "I think we're done here."

"Yes," Finn said as he gathered up the shovel and oilcloth. He rolled the shovel in the cloth and tied them to the back of his saddle. Next, he easily lifted Maureen onto the saddle and quickly mounted up behind her. "I can't wait to hear your story when we get back," he whispered in her ear. She stiffened, and he had a feeling it was going to be a long story.

Their wagons came into sight and dread filled her. Of course, she couldn't tell him everything. She wasn't even sure how to start. John said something about Finn having a price on his head from being a Fenian. She wished she never heard it. Finn might think her a threat.

She wished she could just ride off, but all she had was Contrary and she'd never make it out of camp with that ornery mule. Finn would find out what a great liar she was and she didn't want him to look at her that way. She sighed. There was really no hope for it. She just had to remember not to mention his problem; it could get her killed.

Finn gently lifted her down but this time there were no smiles. His face was grim and her stomach felt as though it was tied into knots.

She busied herself with building up the fire and putting the coffee on to boil while Finn took care of Justice. She put the beans back on to heat and sat down next to the fire. She had to clasp her hands in front of her on her lap to keep them from shaking. Where to begin? How much to tell him? He could get money by turning her in. Not nearly as much as he was probably worth.

She gazed at him. No, he wouldn't turn her in. He fought for the Irish cause so they could be free. He'd understand her plight. Wouldn't he? She could only hope.

Finally as the sun began to set, he sat next to her. "Something you want to tell me, lass?"

"Yes and no. Telling you could get me sent back into a bad

situation, and I need to know you won't turn me in. I barely got away unharmed, and it's been sheer terror at every turn that someone would find out who I am and report me. I'm bound and determined to make a life for myself. A life as a free citizen. A life without papers that state I belong to someone else."

Finn cocked his head as he stared at her. "You have another husband?"

She gave him a sad smile. "If only it was that easy. In Ireland, my family's house was burned for not paying the Lord of the Manor his taxes. We'd always paid on time but in the end that didn't matter. The English soldiers tried to run me down with their horses to take me to the big house. I never ran so fast in my life. Nothing good ever came from being taken to the manor house. Disgrace was always what it ended in and I swore not me. I made it to the woods where other kinsmen were hiding, and they hid me as well." She chewed on her lip and tried to judge what he was thinking, but his face remained expressionless.

"We were left with nothing. They burned all the crops and took our livestock. My brother took a severe lashing for my escape. It had been a bad year for many, and you could see the telling smoke in the sky everywhere you looked. There were too many of us trying to beg for food. There simply wasn't enough for people to give and feed their own families. We all understood." Emotion swelled, threatening to get the better of her as she recalled those awful days.

"I reunited with my family as soon as the soldiers left. We began to walk from town to town, hoping that we'd find something. Once in a while, we'd find some half rotten food or moldy bread. People even started eating grass trying to survive. I had to dress as a young lad to avoid detection. Then we heard about indentured servants in America. It sounded like a grand idea. My youngest brother had already died of starvation, and I couldn't stand to bury another member of my family. I became certain as an indentured servant I could send most of my money back home." She blinked back tears of frustration.

"I dressed as myself and was accepted right away. I felt proud to have found a way to help my parents and family. But that's not how it worked. The ocean crossing was almost unbearable. We were locked in the bottom of the ship. Many of the girls were taken at night and used. I was constantly sick, and the one night I was taken, I was sick on the sailor's boots. He kicked me good, but it saved me. Some didn't make it. I was lucky I did."

She took a deep breath and stared into the distance. "I was settled into a nice home in Missouri with a Mr. and Mrs. Jones and their two boys Clay and Adam. They owned me for five years to pay off my passage and fee."

"That's a long time to belong to another."

She shrugged. "It was."

"But they are after you?" His brow furrowed.

"They wanted me to stay and threatened to extend my indenture papers for two more years, and I took off." She closed her eyes. There. She'd told him the truth except for the very last part. He didn't need to know she ran off after only three years.

"'Tis a sorry story and my heart goes out to you. You were lucky to get away," he sighed.

They sat in silence until the sun went down.

"Tell me about Malcolm," he asked. "How did you make him up and get 640 acres of land?"

"I found a family, the O'Briens, to take me on the Oregon Trail with them as long as I worked. I told them my husband was already in Oregon waiting for me. Mrs. O'Brien died trying to bring her child into the world and the wee one died too. After that, Mr. O'Brien seemed to have lost his will to go on. One morning I woke and when I looked under the wagon, he was gone. We all searched for him but there was no trace of the man."

She shrugged. "Finally we just couldn't take more time looking for him and the wagon master told me I had a choice. I could stay and keep looking though he didn't think I'd find Mr. O'Brien or I could drive the wagon and consider it mine. It almost felt like stealing, since I'd told so many lies already but Mr. O'Brien was nowhere to be found, so I drove the rest of the way. A very nice man lost his wife on the crossing and we got to talking about how he'd planned on the 640 acres, but he didn't want to get remarried just yet. We struck a deal. He'd be my pretend husband with a pretend name in this town, and I'd do the same for him the next town over."

Finn nodded, his lips twitching into a half smile. "Very smart idea."

She shook her head. "I'm thinking it is a common idea. I bet that man we buried wasn't even a Cleary; he was fishing to see if I really had a husband and if not he planned to steal all my land."

Finn's mouth dropped open. "You're very smart for a lass."

Her eyes widened. "For a lass?"

"Kidding, I was. You are wise to the ways of the world for someone so young. It's a shame all you've been through. After I finish my cabin, I'll help you with yours. Of course I'm too tall to stand in the one you have planned but…" He laughed.

"I cut down as many trees as I could. I saw how far behind you I was and figured as long as I fit it would be fine." She smiled. Her heart felt lighter than before the English soldiers burned down her house. "I will take you up on your offer, Finn Langley." She put out her hand and they shook. Something inside her tingled at his touch. It was a very strange occurrence to be sure and she tried to figure out if she liked it or not. She couldn't come to a decision.

"I do have something else I would ask of you." She glanced off into the distance. "I need to know how to shoot my rifle." Her face heated. "I meant to learn but I never really had the need until I settled here alone. Many a night I'd stare at it wishing I knew how to use it. I vowed to figure it out myself but…"

Finn grinned until a dimple showed on his cheek. "It would be my pleasure. You haven't been able to hunt?"

"I can fish and I'm good with snares and I have a sling shot. Use what you can, I always say but I need to protect myself and to do that I need the rifle."

Finn cocked his brow and she smiled. "You're resourceful. I'd be happy to teach you after our days' work is done. We can start tomorrow."

"Thank you. It's getting late, and I'm sore from today."

Finn drank the rest of his coffee. "Have a good night, Maureen."

She watched until he crossed to his side of the stream. Then she quickly cleaned the dishes and groaned as she climbed into her wagon. It was a comfort to have Finn so close. She fell asleep as soon as her head touched her pillow.

CHAPTER THREE

Finn wiped the sweat off the back of his neck with a towel. The mornings and nights were getting colder but the afternoon sun kept a working man warm. The sturdy walls of his cabin were going up. It was a slow process, but Maureen's help was much appreciated. She was mighty strong for such a small lass.

She was also a fast learner and asked many a question. When the sun shone on her red hair, he couldn't help but think it looked glorious. She wore a bonnet in the afternoons but in the mornings, he couldn't seem to stop staring at her. Her skin was like porcelain and her eyes reminded him of blue storm clouds. Her smile brightened the world and soon enough he found himself wondering what it would be like to kiss her.

His thoughts drifted back to Maureen's tale of indenturing herself. Her words had truly touched him. How had she found the strength to sell herself into slavery for the sake of her family? And on what grounds had the family she'd worked for, been able to threaten to extend her tenure in indentured servitude? A frown pinched his forehead as doubt crept in. He'd taken her story at face value when she'd told it, but the more he thought about it, the more he began to wonder if she had left something unsaid. She was holding something back.

"Won't your family be worried when they don't hear from you?" he asked, breaking the silence, hoping she might open up to him.

She looked up from the log she was finishing notching. "I wasn't allowed to get in touch with them when I was turned into a slave. Now, I'm afraid to give away my location." Despair and something undefined flashed in her eyes. "I'm not even sure where they are."

"When we get a chance I'll find them and I'll make sure you can get a letter to them."

She stood and put her hands on her hips studying him. "Who are you, Finn Langley?"

He spread his hands in front of him. "What you see is who I am. I'm a simple man."

Tilting her head, her eyes narrowed a bit. "You wouldn't be fibbing would you? I have a feeling that you're not so simple."

"I was a political man in Ireland," he admitted somewhat reluctantly, "and the English weren't so fond of me. When I found myself with a price on my head, I needed a new start and here I am."

"We're both starting over."

"You could say that." He smiled at her. "Nothing wrong with starting over."

Maureen nodded and sat down. She quickly went back to work. She knew more than she was letting on. He'd have to keep an eye on her. She'd heard John blurt out he was a wanted man. He thought he could trust her, but the price on his head could set her for life. The money would tempt Saint Patrick, himself.

"Rifle lesson after we're finished?"

He looked up at the sun. "I'm thinking we should have them earlier in the day. It's getting darker earlier. How about a few minutes after each noon meal?"

She glanced at him and nodded as a pretty smile crossed her face.

MAUREEN WAS A NERVOUS WRECK. Finn had his well-muscled arms around her guiding the rifle in her hands and his warm breath caressed her neck. It was near impossible for her to concentrate. She aimed at the big tree trunk they were using for target practice and pulled the trigger. She had no idea if she hit it or not. The kick from the rifle pushed her farther into his arms. "Oh, my!"

She pushed away, reloaded, pulled the trigger, and went flying back again. "If you weren't behind me I'd be flat on my back."

"I want you to get the feel of shooting before we work on your stance. You'll be shooting by yourself soon. I promise."

Shrugging, she did it all over again, time after time until Finn announced it was time to go back to work. Her shoulder hurt like the very devil, but she refused to let him know. He'd probably stop the lessons if he knew how bruised she was bound to be.

Later that evening, she put a cloth in cold water and pressed it against her shoulder. It was black and blue, and how she missed her mother's healing ointments. But the cold compress would have to do. She wrapped it so it would stay in place and pulled her biscuits from the fire. The smell of the rabbit stew made her stomach growl, yet no matter how hungry she was, she couldn't help but wonder if her family had anything in their bellies that night.

Finn joined her and poured them both coffee as she doled out the rest of the meal.

"Are you all right?" he asked.

She summoned up a smile. "Of course." She took a bite of the stew and nodded. "Just right, I do believe."

His stare unnerved her.

"What? Is something wrong?"

"You never complain, do you?"

She furrowed her brow. "What do you mean?"

"You're as hurt as a bird with a broken wing, yet you'd rather I didn't know." A smile played on his lips. "I admire your courage, but I'll need to look at your shoulder."

Her jaw dropped. "How did you know?"

"It's been a while since I trained—I mean taught someone to shoot, and I forgot a person of your size would feel the kickback from the rifle more intensely." He stood. "I have something you can put on it."

She watched his fine form cross to his wagon and back.

"I need you to unbutton your dress."

"I certainly will not." She crossed her arms in front of her.

He pulled his crate closer to hers. "I'm not interested in seeing anything else besides your shoulder."

She felt as though she'd been kicked in the gut. Didn't all men like to see a woman's breasts? She heaved a sigh and began to unbutton her dress and hesitantly slipped her arm out of her sleeve. She looked away as he unwrapped her improvised bandage.

He sucked in a sharp breath through his teeth. "For the love of all that's holy, why didn't you say something? This is three times as bad as I suspected."

She stiffened and bit her lip to keep quiet. He opened a jar of some foul-smelling stuff and began to dab it on her.

"Don't move, I want to give it a minute before I rub it in. Meanwhile, I'll make you some tea to take away the pain."

She nodded. Her shoulder was pained but not as painful as her heart was. She knew she enjoyed Finn, but really caring for him and wanting him to return her feelings had snuck up on her. She'd found him attractive from the start, but when had the deep feelings come to be? Most marriages seemed to come about due to need or convenience from what she could see. She was the type whose feelings ran deep, and now that she'd acknowledged them, she hurt.

He knelt in front of her and lifted her chin with his finger. "Hey, the pain will go away. Let me rub this in."

She nodded as her eyes watered. Let him think it was her shoulder that upset her. She'd never want him to know how she really felt. If she really tried, she'd be able to change her feelings. How hard could it be? Many woman were told by their families who to marry and they did it. They survived, somehow.

Next, he poured her tea and handed it to her. "Sip this. It'll take away some of the pain and make you a bit drowsy. I'll make sure the campsite is cleaned. I was thinking, I have some supplies I need to get in town. Why don't I go tomorrow and give you a day to rest?"

He didn't wait for her answer. He began to clean and then he suddenly stopped. "I'll lift you into your wagon. Will you be able to manage getting into bed?"

She nodded. She tried to feel nothing as he lifted her into his strong arms. She tried not to breathe in his scent of pine and campfire. She tried not to stare at his handsome profile. He gently put her in her wagon and bid her good night. She tried not to cry as her hope for a relationship vanished but she had to grab a pillow to muffle the sounds.

The next morning it was so quiet, she became uneasy until she moved. A throbbing ache tore through her shoulder. She yelped in pain as she managed to sit up, leaning against the wooden side of the wagon. She should have slept in her clothes. It would have made today easier. She drew her nightgown over her head and gulped when she saw how deeply bruised she was. Taking a deep breath, she pulled on her dress. It was only a bruise. She'd worked with injuries before.

She cautiously climbed out of her wagon and was pleased to see coffee and what looked like oatmeal ready. She helped herself to both and stared at Finn's cabin. She'd be able to do some chinking today. It was important to fill in the cracks between the logs to keep the cold out. What if they ran out of time and weren't able to get her cabin done?

Well, she had her wagon. Others lived through the winters in their wagons, somehow. She could do it too.

As the day passed, she began to grow worried. What if Finn had been recognized? He wouldn't be coming back if he had. Maybe she should go after him. She put more of the foul cream on her shoulder and saddled Contrary. She had a bad feeling, and she knew not to dismiss a feeling so strong. After a few tries she got the mule to go in the right direction.

THE OLD STAINED mattress in the town jail cell was lumpy and likely filled with vermin. Finn gritted his teeth against the thought of what might be crawling around him as he lounged on it, trying to appear nonchalant. A big burly man with jet-black hair and beard smiled heartily at him.

"Caught me a fine fish," Jinks Clod announced. "You're such a stupid man. You didn't even change your name."

Finn kept his mouth closed. He couldn't incriminate

himself if he was silent. Besides, he'd decided to save his charm for the judge. What would Maureen think? She'd probably worry the night away. Was she safe? Just thinking of her had him longing for her fresh smile. She'd gotten under his skin but he couldn't think about her now. He had his own neck to save...again.

"Hey, sheriff, when do I get paid?" Jinks yelled.

The office was small, and Jinks' voice boomed causing the sheriff to frown. "Paid? We don't pay until we have every bit of evidence. If he's from another country it could take about a year or so I expect."

Jinks took a step toward the sheriff. "Now see here!"

"One more outburst, Mr. Clod, and I'll lock you up and let Mr. Langley go." The sheriff put his feet up on his desk and leaned back. "I have a telegraph sent asking about you too."

Jinks frowned. "I'll be staying at the saloon. Don't worry, I'll be around each day to make sure my money, I mean Langley is safe." He glared at Finn before he left.

The sheriff walked to Finn's cell. "You haven't said very much."

"Nothing to say. He got the wrong man, and all I can do is wait until it's all straightened out."

The door opened and in walked a surprisingly disheveled Maureen. Her bonnet, tied around her neck, hung down her back and half of her hair was falling down. Her eyes looked stormier than ever. She ignored the sheriff and rushed to the bars of Finn's cell.

"Not again! When are people going to stop mistaking you for that other Finn?"

His jaw dropped but he let it play out.

"I don't know," he said with a shrug.

"Sheriff, I've known Finn for most of my life. He's been in

America for fifteen years. The other Finn is fairly new in America from what we can tell."

"And you are?" the sheriff asked as he took his feet off his desk and stood.

"Oh my I forgot my manners. I'm Maureen Cleary. My parents Maureen and Malcolm both died recently leaving me their land. My land is next to Finn's. Finn was supposed to travel the Oregon Trail with us, but he was delayed and Daddy refused wait. Near broke my heart, but I had to go with my family."

"What train did you travel with?"

"Captain John Marshall's, sir."

"Yes, I know him. He went on to Washington Territory for some new adventures. I can check with the land office. When did you claim the land?"

"My daddy did at the beginning of September of this year."

The sheriff nodded. "Finn, when did you file your claim?"

"Eighteen days ago."

"We're getting married and joining our land," she burst out. Her eyes widened she hadn't intended to say that.

The sheriff cocked his head sideways. "I'm leaning toward believing you. Who in their right mind wouldn't have changed their name with a price on their head? Plus this little gal seems honest enough. I'm going to the land office and check a few things out." He walked out the open door.

"What are you doing here?" Finn asked, annoyed that she'd put herself in danger.

"Rescuing you. Don't you dare lecture me. I had to ride Contrary all the way here. I thought I'd be fine but the pain in my shoulder is almost too much to bear. And don't you dare make me cry!"

Her hands held on to the bars and he stepped forward wrapping his hands around hers. "I didn't mean to yell. I just don't want you to go down with me. Take my cabin. You can nail the canvas from my wagon over it for now as a type of roof. Use anything you need from my wagon. I don't want my things to end up seized when they ship me off. There is money enough buried under the right corner of the cabin, the front corner, to hire someone to finish the cabin."

A lone tear trailed down her face. "You aren't going anywhere. We both are from County Cork. Our families settled in Dustin, a small town outside St. Louis. Both our parents were struggling farmers. We'd decided to make a new start and we are getting married. That's the story."

He stared into her eyes. She had so much inner strength. Her plan just might work. "You don't want to marry me."

"Finn, I've found in life there are a great many things we do because it's for the best. Don't worry about it, really."

He swallowed hard. It wouldn't be fair to saddle her with his problems. "I don't think I want to marry you."

The sheriff returned with a short man dressed in black, carrying a bible. "Good news! The preacher is in town. You two can get married now."

Dang! Maureen wouldn't even glance in his direction. He wasn't going to get a chance to tell her the reason he didn't want to marry her.

"Yes, yes I'm very pleased to be able to do such a service. Will the young man have to stay behind bars?" the preacher asked.

Drawing the key out of his pocket, the sheriff opened the cell door. "That's the deal. You join the couple and they can join their land and hopefully I won't have a reason to have them in my office again."

Finn walked out of the open door. He stared at Maureen but she still refused to look at him.

"Now, I need you two to stand side by side." The preacher

waited for them to do as instructed. He opened his bible. "Dearly Beloved..."

Finn couldn't keep his attention on what the man was saying. Why did he say that to Maureen? It didn't bode well for a new life for them. Heck, she thought he didn't want her. Perhaps he could explain...

There was silence, and he swallowed hard. He was supposed to repeat after the preacher. Finn recited his vows and listened as Maureen unhappily whispered hers. He didn't have a ring but he did have a bit of lace he kept to remember his mother by. Reaching into his pocket, he drew it out.

"I wish I had a ring, Maureen. All I have is this bit of Irish lace of my mother's. I carry it with me always. I'd be honored if you'd do the same."

She glanced at him and he could see the tears swimming in her eyes. She nodded and took the piece of lace. "I suppose we should go home now."

He smiled at her. "After I go to the land office and enter our claim."

"Of course." She walked out the door before him. "I'll wait here with Contrary."

"I'll be as quick as I can." He touched her hand and was surprised how cold it was. At least she didn't pull away.

FINN WHISTLED a tune as he came out of the land office. He looked like a very happy man indeed. Maureen held the reins to her mule and waited for him to join her. "You're certainly happy." Her voice had an edge to it but she couldn't help it.

"We are the proud owners of 1280 acres of land, my dear."

"How did you manage that? I didn't think they'd give you more. I thought they'd just join our land."

"Mrs. Cleary owned 640 acres and poor Finn only owned

320 acres. But I'm now a married man so I get 640 acres too." He looked entirely too pleased with himself.

"You cheated, didn't you?"

"Not entirely. I just didn't tell the clerk that Mrs. Langley and Mrs. Cleary was the same person. I didn't want to ask the rules in case it didn't go my way."

She narrowed her eyes. "I wonder if you're a man to be trusted. Do you often bend the rules to your benefit?"

Finn took the reins from her and then he took her hand in his. "I need to get Justice. He's at the livery. I do admit I've had to live by the seat of my pants a good deal of the time, but I want to settle down, with you, *a ghrá*."

"Don't be using sweet Irish on me. I'm not your love." She sighed. "Let's get back home. I've had enough excitement for one day."

They rode side by side to their land. Their land, oh dear Lord, she was a married woman now. What did Finn expect from her? She frowned. She hardly knew him. How was she supposed to lay with him? She groaned out loud.

"Are you all right?"

"No for various reasons, but right now it's my shoulder. It's not easy to guide Contrary."

Finn drew a bit closer to the mule and plucked Maureen right out of the saddle. His hands felt strong and before she knew it, she was seated in front of him.

"Lean back against me, *a ghrá*. I'm sorry I forgot about your shoulder. I'll take good care of you, Maureen." He released a sigh. "Imagine me married to such a beautiful colleen as you."

She was about to take him to task for calling her his love again, but she didn't have the energy. It probably wouldn't do much good.

"Imagine all the land you now own." She sighed heavily.

He chuckled. "The land is just a bonus. I have my freedom, and that is dearer than all the land in the world. I'm sure you of all people can understand that."

She leaned back against his hard, muscled chest. "I do understand all too well. I've changed my name enough times now; I hope I can no longer be tracked down. It's awful having to look over your shoulder all the time. With each stranger I meet I'm wary they are there to take me back."

"You've a husband now. I'll protect you with my life if necessary."

"Things aren't that way in America."

"Why would you think that?"

She shrugged. "Just an observation. Women only seem to be valued for the amount of work they do. And the number of children they have, especially boys."

He kissed the side of her neck, causing her to shiver. "Sometimes people get married out of necessity. Maybe they don't feel the need to show love. Maybe they have no love to give. I'm sorry for them. A heart full of love is a grand thing indeed."

"You sound as though you speak from experience. Did you have a girl you had to leave behind in Ireland?" Her body stiffened. She really didn't want to know.

"Look, we're just about home. Now the new piece of land is mostly timber. I know there are plenty of trees in this part of Oregon. I say we don't touch the trees. With new towns being built, the timber will be worth a lot of money someday. Wouldn't it be something if we build this land up enough to be able to leave a legacy to our children?"

Nodding, she was relieved he changed the subject, but she'd gotten her answer all the same. Who was the girl? Was she pretty? Did they grow up together? Was he pining for her? She'd probably never know. A future of their own, a future without starvation and Manor Lords a future of freedom for their children would be the greatest gift.

At least she and Finn seemed to get along so far. That was a wonderful first step. As they rode toward Finn's cabin, her heart beat faster. Finn's things were strewn all around the area. Shifting in the saddle, Finn quickly drew his sidearm.

"Stay on Justice. I'm going to have a look around." Finn carefully dismounted and handed her the reins. "If there's trouble, ride off toward town."

Her words caught in her throat. She nodded and watched him cautiously walk toward his wagon. In short order, though, he came back for her. He held his arms up and she slid into them. His nearness did strange things to her stomach.

"It looks like a bear was here. I found bear prints, and the meat I had is gone. I'm just glad the wagon is still standing." He took a step back from her and his expression grew serious. "Don't go far without your rifle. Next time we're in town, I'll buy you a gun. Bears are nothing to fool around with."

"I've never seen one close up. I've seen bear heads mounted on walls and of course bear rugs. I'll be careful." She looked around to be sure the bear wasn't anywhere near. "I have left over stew I can heat up for supper." She crossed the stream and when she got to her wagon her heart sank. Her canvas had holes caused by claw marks. Her pot of stew was on the ground and when she picked it up, she could see it had been licked clean. Her sack of sugar lay open and spilled onto the ground with half of it covered in ants.

"He was here too!" she yelled.

Finn was at her side immediately. "Must be a younger bear. There would have been more damage if the bear had been full-grown. The prints weren't the largest I've seen."

"I'm not going to feel safe sleeping here," she said and then immediately wished she could take her words back. "I'm not suggesting we sleep together. I…"

Luckily, Finn didn't laugh at her. She was ready to push him away if he had. "We can share my wagon without actually having—"

"Don't say it. I'm a good Christian woman, and I don't want to talk about it." Her face heated. "Well I'd best get this cleaned up so the rest of the bears don't feel like they've been invited to supper."

Finn tilted his head. "How'd you get your wagon here in the first place?"

She got down on her hands and knees and began to scoop any clean sugar into a pot. "I had two oxen that pulled it here, and then I sold them. I didn't think I'd need them. Perhaps I should have kept them. It would have made hauling logs easier."

Finn nodded. "I sold my oxen too. I already had Justice. Do you need help or would you rather I start supper?"

"I'm starving." She frowned.

"What's wrong? I can cook."

"I was thinking of the people back in Ireland. Compared to them, I've never starved here in America. I've had to go a day here and there without food but nothing like how I lived there. Sometimes I feel guilty living so well while they're languishing."

Finn knelt and put his arm around her. "We'll soon make enough money for you to send to your family. Plus they have one less mouth to feed without you there."

"I don't even know where they are anymore." Tears filled her eyes.

"You can write to one of your old neighbors that didn't get burned out. People tend to keep track of others."

She tried to give him a smile. "You're so right. Go make me some food. I'll finish up here."

Finn stood and went to his side of the stream. Though really, there wasn't a his or her side anymore, she supposed.

It was all theirs. For just a moment, a finger of longing stabbed her heart, and she wondered what it would have been like had he married her because he shared her feelings. But her problems were nothing compared to those of others and she needed to remember to have a grateful heart.

CHAPTER FOUR

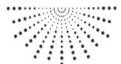

Finn sat by the fire longer than he'd have liked. Had he given her enough time to get settled into bed? He'd moved most of his things into her wagon for now so they'd have plenty of room to sleep together in his. They weren't going to have a wedding night but for some reason he was starting to sweat. She did expect him to stay on his side of the wagon, didn't she?

He was as nervous as a lad still in knickers. After a few more minutes, he stood and climbed into the wagon. Maureen was lying with the covers pulled up tightly to her chin, and she watched his every move with her eyes wide. She reminded him of a scared spinster. He quelled the impulse to laugh. Her beautiful red hair was in a single braid. For a moment, he pictured himself letting her hair fall loose around her head and shoulders.

"I'd thought you'd be sleeping. I waited so you wouldn't have to worry." He took off his boots and noticed how much dirt he'd tracked in. "I guess I should take these off outside from now on." He glanced in her direction. Her face was pale, and she was biting her bottom lip. Were her knuckles so white from holding onto the quilt too tight?

He waited until she finally gazed at him. "I don't expect a wedding night. I want us to get to know each other better first."

She cocked her brow. "What if you don't like me once you get to know me?"

A smile tugged his lips. "I already like you. I want you to feel comfortable. You look as frightened as a calf that lost its mother. Frightened but brave at the same time. It's a lovely combination on you."

"I'm sorry. I'm—"

"Hold on. There is nothing to be sorry about. I'm going to get undressed now. You can turn your back if you like." She turned so fast he wanted to laugh loud and hard, but he just smiled instead. He finally got comfortable under his quilt. "I'm all set. Good night."

It took a few minutes but she lay on her back and peeked at him. Her eyes widened. "You're not wearing pajamas?"

"I have pants on." He couldn't hold it in anymore, and he laughed and laughed. The more he laughed the madder she looked. "I'm sorry. I'm just nervous. Good night *a ghrá*." He waited for her to tell him she wasn't his love, but she closed her eyes instead.

THE NEXT MORNING Finn put his arm out and realized Maureen wasn't there. She sure was an early bird. He sat up and stretched his arms above his head and looked out the back of the wagon. Maureen stood there staring at him and then she abruptly turned her back. His lips twitched. It wouldn't be healthy for him to laugh again. His shirt lay at his feet, and he put it on before he climbed out of the wagon. He then grabbed his boots and put them on.

"It's getting colder and colder," Maureen commented as she made hoe cakes. She'd mentioned she had some syrup she'd been saving to go on them.

"I guess I'll have to work faster to get the cabin done." He squatted down and grabbed the coffee pot. "Do you need a refill?"

"I'm fine, thank you. It should go quickly with the two of us working on it. I think bears are a good incentive to work faster."

He stood with his cup in his hand. "Very true. I saw that you have a cook stove in your wagon. How'd you get it over the mountains?"

"I didn't. It was by the side of the trail not too far from town. I had my *husband* put it in my wagon. He was a nice enough man, but too broken by the loss of his wife."

He sat and stared out into the distance. Was it wrong to be happy that man had been too far into his grief to want Maureen? As Maureen handed Finn his plate of hoe cakes with syrup, he smiled. "I think I've died and gone to heaven."

She sat and took a bite. Her eyelids fluttered down for just a moment. "Oh yes, this was worth saving."

"Thank you for breakfast. I'm going to start on the cabin."

"I'll join you as soon as I clean up here."

Finn nodded, stood, and went to his pile of logs. He needed to notch some more before he could continue building. He worked until he felt the sun on his shoulders. Where was Maureen? He furrowed his brow. She'd been gone a long while.

Worried, he went to her wagon, and discovered the dirty dishes were gone. He walked down the stream and he didn't see her there. He walked a bit farther along the water and finally spotted the clean dishes but not Maureen. Fear clutched at his heart. Where was she?

He called her name a few times, but she never called out

in return. Panic raced through him as he searched the grounds for clues. He found her footprints and some small bear track. Cubs! Dang, there must be an angry mama bear around.

As he tilted his head back to look up to the skies, he spotted Maureen high up in a tree to his right. Taking a deep breath, he let it out slowly. His relief was momentary as his anger took over. "Didn't you hear me calling? Didn't you see me searching?" His voice was intentionally gruff.

"I didn't want the bear to come back." It was a lame excuse.

"I was standing right here with a rifle and my sidearm. Come on down."

He watched as she climbed down with great agility. He lifted his arms to her, but she ignored him and fell to the ground. She got to her feet before he could help her, but his sharp hearing caught her slight moan.

"Why wouldn't you let me help you down? You hurt your shoulder again didn't you?"

Her jaw dropped as she put her hands on her hips. Her eyes flashed in anger. "I could have been eaten alive, and you have the nerve to be upset with me? Don't you think I was scared?"

"Scared witless, yes." He shook his head.

She bent down, grabbed her dishes and the pot and marched off without a word. Finn stood there, taking a few deep breaths and trying to calm himself. She didn't have the proper respect for nature, and she surely had no respect for him. He knew what his father would do, and his father had told him it was the man's duty to teach a wife the way of things.

He stroked his chin. She needed to learn. He walked back to his wagon and saw that Maureen had put all the dishes away and was sitting on a crate with her arms folded in front of her. She had a sour look on her face as if he'd done something.

"Do you realize how dangerous it is out in those woods?" His voice got louder with each word. "Have you no feelings for how I felt looking for you only to find you right above my head?"

She turned her back on him. He shook his head; it was decided. She needed some good old-fashioned discipline, and it was for her own good.

He sat down. "Come here lass." He tried to keep his voice even.

Turning she gave him a frown but did as he said. She gasped in surprise when he pulled her over his lap. She must have realized his intent because she began to struggle.

Finn lifted her skirts and bared her bottom. "This will hurt me more than you." He slapped her buttocks once, twice, three times and more until it was nice and red.

She screamed, wriggled, and made all kinds of threats to kill him. Finally, she was able to kick him, hard, and when he loosened his hold, she rolled off his lap into a heap on the ground.

Narrowing her eyes at him, she yelled. "If you ever lay a hand on me again, I'll cut that hand off and feed it to the bears!" She stood up, righted her skirt, and climbed into the wagon.

MAUREEN DIDN'T KNOW what hurt more, her rear end or her pride. They both smarted. How dare he? She wasn't a child who needed to be punished. She'd just been traumatized by the bear and then again by her supposed husband. She lay on her left side. It was the only comfortable way for her to lie.

She'd seen her share of abusive husbands and fathers all her life and now she managed to have married one.

Her heart sank. She hadn't realized how high her hopes were for a good marriage until it all came crashing down. He'd tricked her into thinking he was a kind and gentle man. Tears started, and they wouldn't stop. Her pillow was soaked before long. He was right about one thing; she had hurt her shoulder again. The pain was worse than before.

She'd work to get the cabin ready before winter. Right now, she didn't have a choice but she would insist on separate beds or maybe a loft just for her. It would be an extra-long winter keeping to herself, but at least she could look forward to the spring when she could resume building her own cabin.

Her father had never spanked her or her siblings. Her face flamed as she thought of Finn seeing her partially naked. He had no right! She'd never be able to face him again. Well, she didn't plan to talk to him again so maybe she wouldn't have to look at him either. She stared at the wagon flap and sighed. It was still morning, which meant it was going to be a long day and she couldn't spend it in the wagon.

She'd do the laundry. She gathered all the clothes she could find and climbed down from the wagon. Next she went to her own wagon, grabbed more clothes and a washtub. After she built up the fire, she filled pails with water, making sure Finn could see her. Her shoulder made a hard chore all the harder.

It was an all day job, and when Finn came for his noon meal, she didn't stop working. She ignored him instead. She was glad when he said nothing but made his own meal, drank some coffee, and left. She felt the heat of his gaze many times but she refused to acknowledge him.

Her shoulder hurt more than before and she realized in her anger she'd made it worse. By the time she'd finished she could hardly use her left arm. At last, she found a moment for herself, and she wet a cloth with the cool stream water and lay it against her shoulder. She'd be of no use tomorrow.

Next, she put the awful-smelling salve on it. If she wanted to eat, she'd best make something. She hauled another pail of water from the stream, and her body screamed when she set it down. Kneading dough was out of the question, but she had some vegetables left. It was hard to cut them, but she did the best she could. She cooked them in the pot for a bit before adding water to make soup. It would have to do.

She wished she had a mirror so she could see what damage the spanking had caused. She felt bruised. She was lucky he hadn't used a belt. Did he have spirits in the wagon? Men were dangerous when they drank. She knew first hand from the family she had been indentured to. She'd often locked her door to keep the mister out of her quarters.

He'd slapped her face a few times leaving such horrible bruises that the priest came by and talked to the mister. After that, he mainly pulled her hair. Did men think because they were bigger they had a right to hit? That didn't seem right.

She ate before Finn was done and then climbed into the wagon and lay on her good side. When he peeked inside, she closed her eyes and pretended to sleep. She could hear his breathing as he watched her for what seemed like an interminable time.

It didn't seem to be much later when he climbed into the wagon. She clenched her teeth and fists. She wanted to hit him and yell at him. It wouldn't help matters, though. She'd need to distance her heart from his since the hurt was almost unbearable. Theirs would be a cold, barren marriage. Loneliness settled around her, and she couldn't shake it. She was better off than she'd been six months ago, but once again she wasn't free. How did other women stand it?

Of course, there weren't many choices for a woman

alone. Marriage had seemed to be the least offensive, but perhaps she'd been wrong. If she'd been qualified to do anything else, she'd have jumped at it. She was probably like most women who wished for love and affection. If they didn't get what they longed for, they just put one foot in front of the other and kept going.

And that was what she would have to do.

CHAPTER FIVE

Finn's heart felt as though it was in a vise. Maureen refused to talk to him. It had been over a week, and boy could that woman carry a grudge. He'd been puzzling over it, and concluded that he must have done it wrong. When his father had spanked his mother, there had been a bit of crying, but then there was laughter behind the closed doors. They come out an hour later looking closer than ever.

He hadn't even used his belt. He'd been easy on her. She was still favoring her left hand and she refused to allow him to look at her shoulder. She helped with the cabin without a word. He'd tell her what to do, and she simply nodded.

Gone were the smiles, the laughter, and the long looks. How was he going to make things better? She had been in the wrong. She could have been killed. He'd had the right of it, and she was just sulking. And he missed her something fierce.

At the sound of horses, he bade Maureen to hide behind the house. For once, she obeyed without a word. Finn had his hand on his gun while he waited for the riders to come into view.

"Howdy," a stocky man with brown curly hair greeted.

Finn nodded. "Hello." He eyed the younger man with him. He was slight of build and had the same hair. Probably the son.

"We're looking for John Cleary. I'm Marcus Cleary, and this is my boy, Doug. John Cleary is our kin. He was last seen coming out this way to talk to our brother Malcomb. We heard he up and married, a lass, Maureen."

Finn widened his stance. "I'm afraid Malcomb is dead, and John did come out to inquire about Malcolm, but he left weeks ago. Maureen is now my wife. Is there anything else I can do for you?"

"If that's the case, we've come to claim Malcolm's land. Women can't own land, everyone knows that." Marcus sneered.

Finn shrugged. "You can ask at the claim office, but here in Oregon a woman *can* own land. She inherits her husband's land when he dies. You have no business here. There's plenty of free land. Like I said, ask at the claim office in town."

"Well, the strangest thing happened. The land office in New Dawn Springs burned down last night. So when I looked at the land map yesterday, this looked to be the best."

Finn narrowed his eyes. "What happened to Abel? He runs the office."

"Dead," Marcus said with a smile. He didn't even try to pretend he had nothing to do with it.

"Malcolm's grave isn't far if you want to pay your respects."

"We're here to get the land. I was hoping the widow would be available to attend to our needs," Doug said eagerly.

Finn stared at Doug with what he hoped was his steeliest

stare. "Like I said, she's my wife." He made his voice as hard as possible.

"Not if you're dead," Marcus said. He acted as though he had the upper hand.

Upon coming West, Finn had practiced a fast draw and he knew he was quicker than most. He wasn't so eager to try his skills, but if he had to—

Maureen quickly rounded the corner of the cabin, rifle in hand, looking dead serious. "I've already buried one Cleary. Another one won't bother me. Malcolm didn't have kin, so get your lying selves off my land." She cocked the rifle.

"Whoo wee, Pa look at her. She sure is purty."

"Doug, shut up." Marcus said, sounding disgusted with his son. "Malcolm was on the outs with the family, but family is still family."

Maureen walked closer with her rifle at her shoulder. "Not if he said he didn't have any. Now I suggest you git. And just so you know, there are copies of the land deeds that were sent to Lafayette. If you had bothered to inquire in town, you'd have known that was the law. Instead, you killed Abel. "

"You don't scare—"

Finn drew his gun and shot a hole clear through Doug's hat. "Like I said, I suggest you leave."

Without so much as a glance at his father, Doug wheeled his horse about and galloped away.

Marcus smiled again, but this time his smile wasn't as confident. "I'm not worried. This will be my land. You can count on it." He slowly turned his horse around and headed in the direction of town.

Maureen threw down the rifle and went running into Finn's open arms. She held on to him so tight he found it hard to breathe. He put a slight bit of space between them before he sheltered her in his embrace. His blood sang as it pumped through his body. It was probably the combination of adrenaline due the confrontation with the Clearys and having Maureen in his arms willingly.

"Why? Why do they want my land? I picked it because of the creek. I can't imagine why there is a constant stream of the fake Clearys showing up wanting land. They didn't even ask much about where John went."

Finn caressed the side of her face with his finger. She was so beautiful yet she didn't seem to know it. "That supposed family is multiplying faster than rabbits. Maybe we need to ride your land and see what all is on it. Have you looked it all over?"

She shook her head. "The farthest I've been is to bury John." She gave him a slight smile. "Contrary isn't the most comfortable ride. Plus she likes to go where she wants best." She suddenly frowned and backed away from him as though she suddenly remembered she was mad at him.

Finn ran his hand through his hair. "Maureen, didn't your pa ever discipline your family? It was common for my da to take my mother into the bedroom, and he used a belt. He used it on all of us."

She lifted her chin. "My father certainly did *not* hit my mother!"

"I bet you know plenty of families that followed the man's rule."

Her brow furrowed, and she walked away. Perplexed, he watched her draw a dipperful of water from the bucket. Then she stared out at the horizon as she slowly drank the water.

His heart thumped in his chest. What she was thinking? Would their rift ever heal?

Maureen turned and walked to his side. "I would prefer talking things out to being spanked. The man I was indentured to use to slap me around, and I swore I'd never allow another man to lay hands on me." She took a deep breath and gazed into his eyes. "I need to know now what your answer is before we consummate this marriage."

Relief surged through Finn as he pulled her into his arms. "I promise never to raise my hand to you again, and if I ever see that man, I will give him a taste of his own treatment." He was a rewarded with the most delicious hug. It was a hug of trust and affection. He tilted her head and then he put his lips over her ripe ones. He deepened the kiss as she put her arms around his neck. He went slowly so not to scare her. When he lifted his head, the dazed look in her eyes gave him all the confidence in the world. He hadn't felt that way in a very long time.

"Does this mean we've made up?" he asked.

Her smile was shy, and her face grew the sweetest shade of pink. "Yes it does. I'm sorry about the tree, but I was scared speechless. I'll let you know right now that I do tend to do things without thinking sometimes. No more spankings on my bare... um, my... Well, no more."

"I promise. Now we need to get back to work if we want a roof over our heads before the first winter. "

She smiled and her eyes were filled with hope and happiness. "Yes let's make our home."

THE NEXT DAY she kept her rifle right within reach. Finn had to ride to town and get some supplies, and she insisted on working on the house. Now every little sound sent her into a panic. After a few hours, though, she took her rifle and sat inside the walls leaning against the logs. She was thankful that Finn had taught her how to use the rifle and the gun.

Just as she began to relax, the sounds of hoof beats drifted in from outside. That sounded like more than one horse! Her heart dropped. All she wanted was to live in peace.

She crept to the opening in the cabin where a door would eventually go and cocked the rifle. She stood and put the butt of the rifle against her pained shoulder ready to shoot. "Hands up you measly cowards!"

"*A ghrá*, it's me."

Maureen put the rifle down and walked out. The reason she'd heard more than one horse became instantly apparent. Finn had brought another horse home. Smiling, she hurried over to meet the new horse. She was a beautiful bay.

"Where'd you get her?"

"In town." He broke into a grin. "She's for you. Her name is Vala."

"Chosen! Yes Vala is a good name. I like it. And thank you." Warmth flowed through her as she patted the horse's neck. It had been a long time since she'd been given a gift.

"It was worth it to see you smile." He jumped down off Justice.

Taking the reins, she walked Vala around the area. "It's a good place to live. You'll like it here, and Justice is a nice horse."

Vala nickered, and Maureen grinned. "Yes, I do believe we'll be friends." Before she knew it, Contrary was following behind. Maureen laughed. She glanced around and caught Finn's gaze. His big grin was heart stopping. His dimple was showing, and it made her stomach feel as though it was flipping over. It was time to put any hard feelings away and work together. Though now the sun had heated things a bit, it had been cold that morning. Winter was on its way.

"Was there any news in town?" She gritted her teeth and waited, not wanting the answer.

"Your 'family' disappeared. In fact, people saw the two unsavory men but swear their name wasn't Cleary. I sat in the saloon for a bit hoping to hear some local gossip about the men or the land. I didn't learn a thing. I did see the sheriff on the boardwalk and he asked how you were."

Her eyes widened as she frowned. "Why? Why would you take a chance by talking to the sheriff? He'll be out here and all will be lost to us." Her heart slammed against her chest at the thought of the sheriff finding out their secrets.

"It's what normal people would do. We want to appear as normal as possible. I've found in America it's the drifters that usually get blamed for most problems. The good local folks never do." He flashed another grin. "I like to study people and situations so I can blend in."

"Part of me wants to call you foolhardy but in fact you're a wise man, Finn Langley. And I thank you for the horse. We can get twice as much work done around here now."

Finn's laugh started as a small rumble that grew deep. "Well we won't be going in circles for a while before we can get any work done."

"Contrary was aptly named."

His laugh filled her heart. She knew she wouldn't be able to stay mad at him for very long. He'd made himself at home in her heart.

"Well, Mr. Langley, we don't have time to waste. We have a house to build."

He let Justice graze but he staked Vala. Contrary never wandered off. She probably couldn't find her way. "Yes we do. Work while the sun shines."

She nodded. "My da used to say the same."

They worked the rest of the day, teasing each other and having a good time. It was hard work and her movements were limited because of her shoulder but she did what she could.

She went to the wagon to get out the ingredients for biscuits. She'd fry up some bacon to go with it and she had some berry jam. It wasn't the best dinner but it would have to do. She then went to the stream and washed her hands. As she walked back to the fire, Finn took her hand and led her to a crate.

"You need to rest that shoulder. I'll make dinner." He took the coffee pot and filled it with water from the stream.

She'd never known anyone like Finn. He was a kind man, except for his punishment, which he'd promised would not happen again. He acted as though he genuinely cared for her, but how could he? He barely knew her. For all he knew, she was putting on a nice, happy face and she was really a shrew inside. She laughed.

"What's so funny?" He glanced at her and their gazes met and held.

"I was just thinking how kind you are."

He cocked his brow. "I see why that would be funny." He went back to making supper.

"I was thinking that you probably think me nice, but for all you know I could be a shrew."

This time Finn chuckled. "You, my lass are many things but a shrew you're not. Though there was a moment or two I wondered."

She huffed a deep breath. "And just what, might I ask, did you find yourself wondering, Finn Langley?"

He gave her a solemn nod. "Well, now, darlin', let me tell you. When we first met and I thought you and your husband were in need of assistance, I wondered myself if it would be foolish to offer as you might be a shrew under your... friendly manners."

"You—" She drew a sharp breath. "You wondered if I was a shrew? Well, have I shown you enough of my true nature now, so you've managed to figure it out?"

"I should say so." Finn shot her an exaggerated wink.

"After all, it's not every woman who threatens her husband to tear off his arm and feed it to a bear."

Heat swamped her face. "That — that was because you…"

He threw his head back and guffawed. "Put me in my place it did."

"So you do think I'm shrewish!"

"Now, did I say that?" He shook his head. "Have I not told you that you are no shrew?"

"Well then, how do you see me?" she demanded.

His chuckle echoed around the clearing as he turned back to cooking without answering.

How infuriating of him not to answer her question. Not knowing what to say next, she kept quiet, watching Finn. He looked to be cooking with ease and experience. He sure was fine of form. His pants outlined the muscles in his legs. Her face heated as she enjoyed him bending over. Suddenly the cold night was getting uncomfortably warm.

He often glanced at her and smiled. She was far too vulnerable of his smiles.

She stood. "I have to… I'll be right back." She walked away until she found a tree to lean against. She closed her eyes hoping her heart would stop pounding. It seemed to take forever before the wind felt chilled again. Men were a complete mystery to her. Her father had been a good man but the English soldiers, the sailors, Mr. Jones, all thought a woman was good for one thing and they were all willing to take her virtue by force. She shrugged.

If her family had been allowed to stay in their home in Ireland she'd probably be married to Sean Murphy by now. It wouldn't have been her choosing. And she was pretty sure Sean was sweet on Lucy but their parents had made the match long ago. Perhaps she'd dodged a bad marriage the day the soldiers came.

It was funny how a person's whole world could change in

an instant. She still needed to tell Finn that she'd lied and hadn't finished her indentureship. He'd think badly of her. Maybe she'd tell him later. Yes later was the better option.

"Maureen? Are you all right?"

"Yes, I'm coming." She was back to normal, but how long would it take before she needed to cool off again?

As soon as she caught sight of him, her question was answered. Not very long at all.

CHAPTER SIX

Two weeks. They'd been married two weeks, and all he'd gotten were a few kisses here and there. He was working on the roof and watching Maureen washing clothes. For him, taking it slow meant two or three days, not two weeks.

Perhaps she was one of those women who didn't enjoy being touched too intimately. It was a shame; she was made for loving and touching. He could hardly look at her before his body responded. It wasn't because he'd been celibate for a while; it was all Maureen. She was beautiful and full of grace, and he couldn't stop gazing at her delectable lips. Her kindness in her heart shone through in everything she did, and she was funny and intelligent. She knew that they were partners, and she did her share if not more. She was a lass to admire, and he was lucky to have her.

The house would be done in a few days, and he planned on a wedding night but how to tell her? What if she balked? He sighed as he swung the hammer. He'd build her a house of her own next year if that was the case. He wanted her too much to be around her and not be able to ever touch her.

He stole another glance, to find her bent over the tub. His breath caught; he could practically see down her dress. Quickly, he looked away. He was a man of integrity, after all. He based his beliefs on what was right and just. He missed Ireland something fierce and wished he was there to continue the fight for a free country. There was still so much to do, but he was on the sidelines now. He still had the passion of a free Ireland inside him and he always would. It was in his blood. But Oregon was his home now.

He had no way of knowing what was going on. There wasn't much news out this way. At least he hadn't been hauled in front of a wall and shot like so many before him had been. The other lads would continue on without him. Maybe someday he'd make enough money to send back to the Fenians. He took a deep breath. For now, he had to get the house done and stop acting like a schoolboy around Maureen.

According to the Donation Land Claim Act, he had four years to build on and cultivate the land and then it was his. He pictured cattle, horses, and wheat to ensure his fortune. They'd have a large vegetable garden. He'd spend the winter making furniture, and if need be he could sell some. Back in Ireland, he'd been considered a craftsman by many. There were acres and acres of timber waiting for when the growth of the territory happened, and he was sure it would. He also had Maureen. A family would be nice to have. Some wee ones running around. Yes, he could have a good life here, God willing.

"Are you out of nails?" Maureen yelled up at him.

He drew his brows together. "What?"

"You've been sitting there for so long, I thought you were out of nails."

He chuckled. "No, I was thinking about our future and about all the wee ones we would have."

Her face pinked adorably as it softened. "Wee ones would be good." She turned and walked back to her washtub.

His jaw dropped and his heart skipped a beat. *Wee ones would be good.* Had he heard her correctly? Maybe she wanted to make the babies now. He started to gather up his tools and stopped. Of course she didn't mean *right* now. This waiting was going to kill him.

That evening Maureen put on her nightgown that had a pretty pink bow on it. Tonight was the night. Her body shivered in excitement. She'd be a real wife. What if it hurt? She remembered hearing that there was pain involved. Wasn't there another way to get with child? Her excitement waned. She did like his kisses and when he held her... Maybe it wouldn't be too bad.

She slipped under the quilts. Soon they'd be sleeping in the cabin, but the wagon had been cozy for the two of them. Now what? Did she just wait? Should she say or do something special? Perhaps she'd hold his hand when he came to bed. That would be invitation enough, if he really did want her. The longer she waited, the more nervous she became. She blew out the lamp and her conviction to become a bride waned.

He sure was taking his sweet time. She stifled a yawn. It seemed as though she'd been alone in the wagon forever. Then it began to rock as he climbed inside. He took off his shirt, and she saw enough to make her mouth go dry. He left his pants on as he climbed under the covers with her.

Her heart beat louder. Surely he could hear it! She hesitated and then reached out her hand. He took it and gave it a gentle squeeze. Her heart leaped, and her body tingled. Then he let go and turned his back to her. She could tell by his heavy even breaths that he had fallen asleep.

She stared at his back most of the night wondering where she had gone wrong. She thought he wanted to… Her heart was bursting with love for him but he didn't feel the same way. He didn't have to say it, she felt it keenly when he turned away from her. She refused to cry though. She'd cry in private. After all, it wasn't his fault he didn't love her. They had been thrown together, and she had let her imagination get away from her. What type of marriage would they have? He'd spoken of children. He must think of having a family as his duty, and maybe he was putting it off.

The pain in her heart was unbearable, but she couldn't make him love her if he wasn't so inclined. Most marriages were probably the same. She'd stupidly thought he cared for her, loved her even. There was no bigger fool than she. She was forever hoping for things that would never be. She had her pride and she'd never let on he'd hurt her. Somehow, she'd have to learn to not love him, but how?

THE NEXT MORNING she woke late, and the coffee was already made and Finn was already up on the roof. She must have stepped over some unknown line. He hadn't even bothered to wake her. Maureen's chest tightened and her heart dropped. Could he not even bear to look at her? She smoothed one hand over her hair. She hadn't gotten much sleep, and she probably looked it.

Quickly, she used some water she'd poured into a basin to wash and then she dressed. She left the wagon and grabbed the coffee pot without a hot pad. It hurt like the flames of hell and she cried out. Hurrying to the stream she sank her hand into it trying to take the pain away. Couldn't she do anything right?

She felt the heat from his body behind her. She wanted to yell at him and tell him to go away and leave her be, but she clamped her mouth shut. She refused to act like a child.

He knelt beside her and she could smell the wonderful scent that was only his. He smelled like fresh-cut wood, pine trees, and leather. It was both pleasure and heartfelt pain to have him so near.

"What happened?" He took her hand out of the stream and examined it. "You burned yourself good. I have some salve."

"Do you have a salve for whatever ails you?"

He gave her a gentle smile. "Probably not everything." He helped her to stand and led her toward the fire.

He probably doesn't have a salve for a broken heart. She sat on the tailgate of the wagon while Finn put salve on her burn and then wrapped her hand in a bandage.

"If you didn't want to work you could have just told me. You didn't need to hurt yourself, *a ghrá*."

His use of the term of endearment squeezed her heart beyond repair. She nodded absently.

He tilted his head as he gazed at her. "Is there something else wrong? If I can help, let me."

An unwanted tear rolled down her face. She quickly dashed it away. "It just hurts is all. I'm tough, I'll be fine in a bit."

She could tell by his expression he didn't believe her. "I'll be up on the roof. I want you to rest, please. It'll be so much warmer when I put the woodstove in and the roof is finished."

"Yes, I bet it will." She stared down at her bandaged hand. What a stupid mistake.

He stood there for another minute and then he walked away, taking her heart with him. Emptiness filled her, a good companion to her pain. She had no one to talk to. No one to ask what she should do. All she could do was pray.

When she was finished, she felt better but her problems were still there except she wasn't alone any longer. She felt a smidgen of hope.

Though it was a struggle, Finn kept his wits about him on the roof. The day was cold and windy, and he couldn't stop glancing at Maureen. She seemed upset about more than a burned hand. He'd never understand women. If only she'd open up to him. He had a feeling he hadn't heard the whole story of her being an indentured servant. They probably worked her hard but he didn't think that bothered her. Maybe that heathen she worked for had taken advantage of her.

He ran his hand through his hair and looked up at the cloudless sky. They'd have to talk. They could have a good marriage, he knew it, but he didn't know how to get past the wall she'd put up. Maybe once they got settled into the cabin. At this rate, maybe he should have put in a bedroom just for her. He smiled. He'd get his fiddle out tonight and play her music from home. Maybe that would make her happy.

Movement in the distance caught his eye. A man on horseback was riding the edges of the property that Finn could see from the roof. What was with that piece of property people were so intrigued with? He needed to spend more time at the pub. The saloon was full of gossip and information. He'd have to leave Maureen alone again, but she knew how to handle a gun now, plus she needed her rest.

Finn watched until the man turned and rode for town. Then he put his tools away and climbed down the sturdy, wooden ladder he'd made.

He walked to the fire and was taken aback by the sadness on Maureen's face. "You look as though you have the world's troubles on your shoulders. Would you like to tell me why you're so sad?"

"I'm fine really. Just a bit homesick." She stared at the ground the whole time.

"There was a rider on your property just a bit ago. I'm heading to town to see if I can get anyone to talk about what's supposedly on that land. You'll be fine here?" He waited for her to look at him but she didn't.

"I'll be just fine. Go and find out what people are after." A scowl creased her forehead. "It's becoming a real problem."

Finn leaned down and kissed her on the cheek. "I'll probably be back late. I'll be at the saloon, and I might have to wait for some of them to get soused before they talk."

She tilted her head up and gazed at him. "You be careful, Finn Langley."

"Aye. I'll be back. Keep warm and keep the rifle with you."

Chewing her lip, she nodded but said nothing.

He filled his saddlebag with a blanket and a canteen of water. Then he saddled Justice. He glanced at her one more time before he mounted the horse and off he went.

Maybe she really was homesick. She'd have been in America for about five or six years. That was a long time. Maybe she could write to her family, maybe a letter would follow them to wherever they'd gone. He'd managed to get messages to his family from time to time. He knew it eased their minds that he was well.

It was a good hour's ride to town. Not really that far at all. He rode up in front of the saloon, dismounted, and tied Justice to the hitching post. The brassy tones of a piano playing what passed for music in these parts along with the voices of men talking loudly to be heard drifted from the building. He smiled at the western batwing doors. It seemed that all the saloons had them. He pushed them open and entered.

The first time he'd been there, he'd expected some rundown place, but the saloon had the shiniest bar he'd ever seen. It ran the length of the room. A mirror hung on the wall behind the bar and the frame looked to be gilded gold. Next to the mirror was a painting of a near naked, busty woman. That frame also looked like it was gold. The tables weren't all marred, and there wasn't a broken chair to be seen. Who owned this bar?

He stood at the bar, and the bartender—a man he'd heard the others call Benny—nodded. He was nicely dressed, but it was apparent if anyone got out of line he'd be able to take a man's head off in one punch.

Benny sized him up then asked. "What'll be?"

"Whiskey."

Benny grabbed a small glass and a bottle of whiskey. He poured it and set it down in front of Finn. "You have a place around here, don't you?"

"Yes. It straddles the stream north of here."

"In that case, you can settle up before you leave. Too many new people coming in and trying to leave without paying." Benny smiled, flashing his gold tooth on his front upper gums.

"Howdy, neighbor," a tall scruffy man to his right said.

Finn nodded in greeting.

"I'm Mesquite and this here is my friend, Cluck." He nodded to a pair of men flanking him. "And that there is Bob."

Finn tensed. "Nice to meet you. I'm Finn." They didn't look like the type he'd want to take home to meet the wife. "You called me neighbor. Do we have property near each other?"

Cluck stepped away from the bar and pushed his way in

between Mesquite and Finn. "Before you ask, Cluck is my name 'cause I used to be a chicken farmer. Not much money in it though. Most people have their own chickens."

Finn had to keep his lips from twitching. Cluck smelled to high heaven. "I was hoping to get hitched to that little red-haired widow, but you scooped her up mighty fast like."

"I guess I can understand why it would seem fast to you, but we'd gotten to know each other and we get on well. It just felt natural to get married."

"Hey, Benny!" Bob called. "More whiskey for the four of us. Finn's buying!"

Benny caught Finn's eye, and Finn nodded. He waited for his whiskey before suggesting they have a seat at a table.

"You fellas have a ranch or something around here?" Finn tried to sound a bit bored as he asked about their home a second time.

"We got land," Mesquite said. I got 320 acres and Cluck got 320 acres and Bob got 320 acres so we have, oh let's see, according to my figuring we have 820 acres all told." He smiled proudly.

Finn waited for one of the other two to correct Mesquite's figuring, but they didn't.

"Where abouts?" He slung back his whiskey.

Bob stared at him. "We own the land next to your pretty wife's. I'm hoping she'll be willing to sell. We plan on a big cattle ranch, but we don't have enough land, and hers is a good piece of property. I rode over that way today. It would go good with our land."

Go Good? What were these yahoos up to? "Well, sorry we're going to keep it. I have plans for it too. It looks like this town is going to be growing, with all the new landowners. We're lucky we got here early enough to get good choices of property."

Bob, Cluck, and Mesquite glanced at each other frowning. Bob stood and walked to the bar. He came back with a bottle of whiskey, most likely put on Finn's tab.

He sat and poured everyone a drink. "Funny thing about the West. You only have what you can hold."

"Hold?"

Bob nodded. "I can tell you're not from around here. You talk all funny like. You need to be able to defend your property to keep it." He stared Finn down.

Finn didn't flinch. He'd stood his ground against British soldiers. These yokels didn't scare him. "I can see the wisdom in it. Where I'm from, folks just place traps with explosives around their property to keep unwanted guests away." He shrugged but held Bob's stare. "I'm not sure if it's legal here but I put a few around anyway."

All three men turned white. He'd bought himself some time at least. Keeping his movements lazy and calm, he refilled his glass. "Can you tell me something? What is on my land that everyone is willing to kill for?"

In mid-drink, Mesquite choked.

Cluck shrugged his shoulders. "Something valuable maybe?"

Finn could tell by Cluck's yelp that Bob had kicked him. "Maybe you're right, Cluck. I'll have to think on it."

And with that, he decided it was time to take his leave. He shoved his chair back, but before he could stand, a pretty saloon girl with long curly blond hair sat down on his lap. Her low-cut gown was the brightest shade of red he'd ever seen.

"Hello, handsome. I haven't seen you in here before. I'm Audra. It's nice to make your acquaintance." She kissed his cheek and started to touch his neck and chest, leaning close and deliberately teasing with a glance down her dress.

"I'm Finn. And I don't want to seem rude, but I have my wife to get home to."

Everyone at the table laughed.

"Having a good time with a saloon girl doesn't count for cheating. Audra could probably teach you a thing or two," Mesquite said. His knowing laugh turned Finn's stomach.

Finn managed to get Audra off his lap without pushing her to the floor. Then he gave the three men a long, intense glare, silently warning them not to mess with him. "I need to get going."

On his way out, he stopped by the bar and settled up with Benny. "Hey, Benny, have you ever heard of anything valuable on the land near the stream?"

Benny glanced around before he answered. "It's rumored outlaws used to use the canyon over there for a hideout and they buried a box of gold intended for the army in there somewhere."

Finn gave him a generous tip. "Thanks for the information."

Finn untied Justice, put his foot in the stirrup, and settled himself in his saddle. Gold was bad news. They'd forever have people trying to find it. People would be willing to kill for it. As he rode home, he wondered if the story was true. Not that it mattered. The important thing was that others thought it to be true. He needed a plan.

The sun had set by the time he got back to Maureen. At first, she gave him the sweetest smile and then she stared at him. He walked closer to her.

"Good to be home."

"Is it? I bet you enjoyed being in town immensely." She stood and crossed her arms.

"Not particularly. I did find out some information though."

She cocked her right brow. "Was that information given before or after she kissed you?"

He frowned. "What are you talking about? I met with three men."

She shook her head. "Oh? Which one of those men was wearing lip stain?"

He groaned and touched his cheek. "It's not what you think. Audra just sat down as I was leaving. As soon as she kissed me, I told her I had a lovely wife at home and I practically pushed her off my lap." He knew he'd said the wrong thing by the anger in Maureen's eyes.

Her jaw dropped and she closed it quickly. "Goodnight." She practically jumped into the wagon.

Finn sighed. So she was the type to jump to conclusions, great, just great. Now what?

He stared into the fire, watching as the flames danced over the logs, rising and falling. A log popped and sent a shower of sparks into the air, and Finn smiled as realization stole over him. Jealous, was she?

MAUREEN QUICKLY PUT her nightgown on and slid into bed. The nerve of that man! Here she was feeling sorry for herself and trying to come up with a plan to fall into his arms while he was getting kissed by some woman named Audra. He even knew the woman's name. Suspicious, very suspicious indeed.

It was a curse. She'd seen it too many times in her life. Men got the drink in them, and all common sense went out the window. Never would she have guessed it of Finn, though. Audra was probably pretty and wearing something more alluring then the dresses Maureen wore. Of course, Audra would also have more experience in man pleasing.

Her shoulders sagged. *She'd* wanted to be pleasing to Finn, but now she didn't want him near her.

Finn climbed into the wagon, and she turned onto her side, presenting her back to him. She listened while he got undressed. He got under the covers, and she tried to stay as still as possible.

A moment later cold feet were on her legs making her jump. She had nowhere to go. She was stuck between the side of the wagon and Finn. To make it worse Finn was laughing.

"Stop it! I'm going to box your ears, Finn."

He wrapped his arms around her and his hands were freezing as well.

"Brr. What do you think you're doing? I've suffered enough indignity already today. You don't need to add to it. Get off me and sleep it off. I'll punch you in the morning. It'll give me something to look forward to."

Finn laughed louder and harder, shaking them both. Ah, my love, I'm flattered you're so mad, but nothing happened. She sat in my lap and kissed my cheek before I even knew it was happening. Like I said, I got her off my lap as fast as I could. The other men said sleeping with a wh… a saloon girl didn't count as cheating but I said it did."

He kissed the back of her neck. "Maureen, I'd never want another. You're the only one for me. I never felt this way about another colleen."

Did he mean it, or was he a fast talker? She hoped he meant it. His kisses made her forget herself. "Finn, I need to think things through and I can't do that with you kissing and touching me."

He loosened his hold on her and took his feet off her. "Anything you want, my love."

It felt nice to be in his arms. Before long, her eyes grew heavy and she drifted to sleep.

She woke early and found herself still in the circle of Finn's strong arms. She felt safe and cherished, but she couldn't trust her feelings when he was near.

He stirred and tightened his hold. "Good morning, my beautiful wife." He kissed her between her neck and her shoulder, tickling her skin with his whiskers and making her laugh. "I'll get the fire going so you won't be so cold." His voice was so tender she decided she'd been wrong about Audra.

Maureen waited until Finn was outside before she dressed. She took a little more care than usual. When she climbed out of the wagon, she was rewarded with a grin that took her breath away.

"I'm sorry about the accusations last night, Finn."

He poured her a cup of coffee and handed it to her. "No harm done."

"Did you find anything else about the land?"

"According to Benny the bartender, legend has it that outlaws buried a box of gold on your part of the land. Supposedly from the army."

She put her hand to her neck. "Oh no. We'll have people on our land forever."

"I was thinking the same thing. We need to come up with some plan where someone finds the box—empty or something. I'll need to find out exactly what type of box it was. Oh if anyone asks I did plant a few explosives around the perimeter of our property."

She opened her mouth.

"Don't ask. I'll tell you later. I want to get that roof done and then go hunting." He leaned in and gave her a long lingering kiss that warmed her insides better than any fire.

She touched her lips while he walked to the cabin. He was a confusing man and she couldn't figure him out. His kiss was a tonic for her, and hopefully she wasn't being a fool.

CHAPTER SEVEN

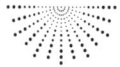

*E*very chance he got during the following week, Finn touched Maureen. Light touches, quick kisses, and standing close to her appeared to be working. She seemed to be softening up to him. She eagerly slept in his arms at night. The cabin would be done in about two days, and he had crafted a bedframe in the little spare time he had. He had Maureen sew a mattress they could stuff with dried hay.

He planned to make their first night together special. But first, he needed to make another trip to New Dawn Springs. He needed more information about the money supposedly buried on their property. He wanted to live in peace and not constantly looking out on the horizon for trouble.

He was busy fashioning a secure door when he decided now was as good as any to go to town. Maureen was making a rag rug for their home.

"I need to find out more about that box and who stole it and where the outlaws are now. For all we know it's a tall tale but people believe it."

Maureen glanced up at him. "Do you want to go and find it for ourselves?"

"No, definitely no. People would kill us for money like that. I've found if you have money, you don't advertise it. You'll live longer."

She looked thoughtful for a moment. "You're right but it sure would be nice to be rich."

"*A ghrá*, remember where we came from. The richest were the most unjust. They felt entitled to take anything they wanted, including another man's wife to warm their beds for a night, and they were always backed by the soldiers. I'd rather sacrifice the money before I became like one of them. My way of thinking is that they wanted to be rid of all Irish." He sighed loudly. "I'm sorry. I feel helpless here when I could be fighting for our freedom."

Maureen stood and stroked his face. "Finn, you did fight. You made a difference. It's just out of your hands at the moment. I'm sure once we're settled and secure you'll find a way to keep helping from here."

He pulled her to a standing position and kissed her. It was a light kiss at first and then he deepened it until he felt her shiver. He could feel her lips turn into a smile. He pulled back, stared into her wide blue eyes, and smiled back. "I should go."

They heard the horses and sprang apart. Finn had his hand on his sidearm as he pushed Maureen behind him. It was the sheriff followed by another man. What did they want?

"Good day, Sheriff," Finn said when they reined in their horses. "What can I do for you?"

"It's your wife we're here to talk to."

Finn felt Maureen stiffen behind him and she let out the softest of whimpers.

A tall man, nicely dressed with brown hair that touched his shoulders pointed to her. "That's Maureen McDonald. I own her, and she ran off."

Finn stepped forward. "Her name was Maureen Cleary and now is Maureen Langley. You have the wrong person."

"Sorry, friend," the tall man said. "I'm Carlton Jones and that woman is *my* Maureen. She still owes me two years plus five days for every day you've been on the run. That's two and a half more years added on." His smile was chilling.

So he'd been right; she had left something out of her story. His heart sank. From her tears, he suspected things were about to get a lot more complicated.

"She also stole a horse," Carlton added.

"I left it at the stable in Independence. You're riding that horse now!" Maureen's eyes opened wide as she realized how much she'd said.

She stared into Finn's eyes. Hers were full of defeat and regret. "I'm sorry I lied. I guess this means we're not married either." Tears began to flow.

The sheriff dismounted and took Maureen by the arm. "Finn, if you have a horse for her to ride into town you'd best saddle it."

Finn nodded. Four and a half years. She owed that bastard four and a half more years. Why hadn't she told him the truth? He felt his dreams disappearing one by one. He got Vala ready, and Carlton grabbed the reins.

"I'm so sorry, Finn. I wish—"

Carlton grabbed Maureen and put her up on the horse. "Hush! You have no more wishes of your own. You only wish what I tell you to wish."

Maureen closed her mouth and lowered her head, staring at Vala's neck. Finn's anger nearly boiled over. His feisty wife had been immediately cowed. She'd been mistreated by that man harsher than she'd let on.

"Hold up, I'm coming with you," Finn growled.

"No can do, Finn," said the sheriff. "You can't interfere and if you do I'll have to arrest you."

Finn stood helplessly while they rode away. Maybe he should shoot both Carlton and the Sheriff out of their saddles, take Maureen and make a run for it, but that would be no kind of life for them. Over four years was a long time to wait, but as far as he was concerned, he was still married.

He sat down on the top step leading to the cabin, took his hat off, and buried his face in his hands. There had to be something he could do. Maureen had said Carlton was starting to make advances on her.

He got up, saddled Justice, and rode to town. He'd do whatever it took, he vowed.

Maureen's tears dried up on the way into town. She didn't want Carlton to think he had a major win by taking her away from Finn. He'd taunt her with her love for Finn for the next four and a half years. Carlton had certainly come a very long way to find her. She wondered what his wife Sadie had to say about that.

Sadie had never wanted Maureen in the first place but Carlton had insisted, and Sadie did everything Carlton told her to do. Theirs was the type of marriage Maureen was trying to avoid. At least she had experienced about six months of freedom.

She'd failed everyone, herself included. They rode to the jailhouse and when she went to dismount, Carlton grabbed her waist and practically threw her to the ground.

The sheriff frowned. "No need to be so rough. Let's get her inside. I have paperwork to do before you can take her."

She stood straight and tall with her head held high as she walked by the gathering crowd. Didn't they have something else to do?

"Hey! Can I have your property?" asked a man who hadn't bathed in at least a month.

"It belongs to my husband." She kept walking.

Did she still have a husband? Her heart felt as though someone was yanking it out of her body, and she wanted cry out from the agony of it.

The sheriff led her to a cell and put her in. The sound of the metal door closing and the lock clicking sent chills up her spine. How had she gotten herself into such a muddle? It was going to be a long journey back to Missouri, and how were they to do so with the upcoming winter? An ache developed in her chest. And how would she be able to live without Finn?

She sat on the old, stained mattress and rested her head against the wall behind her. She'd have to learn to live with her actions. She'd been wrong to leave, and she'd been wrong in not telling Finn the truth. This muddle was of her own making. She knew it was wrong leaving before her indentureship was completed. Now she had two and a half years added.

Carlton had a gleam in his eye. "You know, Sheriff, if she belongs to me then so does her property. How much do I own now?"

"None," the sheriff said without looking up from his desk. He was searching for some papers.

"Now see here—"

"Listen, Mr. Jones, you're lucky I've gone along with getting Mrs. Langley for you. Her marriage is legal. Her property now belongs to her husband."

"But if I had been here, she wouldn't have been allowed to get married. She can only do what I say she can do. She is a servant, and I own her," Carlton said, puffing out his chest.

The sheriff narrowed his eyes. "You keep saying you own

her, but we don't own people here in Oregon Territory. It's a free territory and we're proud of it."

Carlton smiled. "For slaves yes but I have a signed contract. I'll need to get headed back East before winter sets in."

"You'll never make it back over the mountains. In fact, I'm surprised you made it here this time of year. You got lucky."

"In that case we'll settle in her cabin. It'll be cozy just the two of us, right Maureen?"

Maureen shook her head. "It's not my cabin. It's Finn's, and it's on his original land. I do have a broken down wagon with a damaged canvas you could use. I don't think it would be very warm though."

Carlton frowned then chuckled. "It'll be warm with the two of us."

The sheriff got up and opened his door. "That's enough of that type of talk, Mr. Carlton. I run a clean town, and I won't have you sleeping with another man's wife. I suggest you go think of another plan. Don't you already have a wife?"

Maureen's body sagged as Carlton walked out the door.

The sheriff shook his head, muttering to himself. Then he turned to her. "I thought it was against the law to have indentured servants. I'm not sure though. The laws of the States and Territories differ in a few areas. He was able to do it, so there must be some type that was legal. I'm going to send a few messages out and see exactly what the law is in this situation. Sorry, but you'll probably be here for a few days. I'll have one of the gals come and bring you fresh sheets and the like. I'm sure Finn will be along soon."

Maureen's body began to shake, and she wrapped her arms around herself. Her worst fear had come true. Why had Carlton come all this way? He'd left Sadie and the children alone? Closing her eyes tight, she tried to block it all out and think of Finn's smile and touch. Even that didn't last long, though, and she wasn't sure how to comfort herself.

Would Finn show up? She wouldn't have blamed him if he washed his hands of her. She'd told him one lie after another, and all he'd ever been was good to her. She should have told him the truth, but fear had stopped her, and now here she was in a stinking cell, alone. The worst part was that she'd hurt Finn.

The door opened, and she immediately stood, her heart jumping in hope that it was Finn. But it was a woman, and Maureen's heart dropped. The stranger wore a warm cape and carried bedding and a basket, all of which she placed on the sheriff's desk.

Her dress was that of a saloon girl, and Maureen didn't know what to think.

"I'm Audra. I brought you sheets and a quilt. They don't get too many female guests in here." She grabbed the bedding and pushed the items one at a time between the bars.

They were clean. "Thank you, Audra. I believe you know my husband."

Audra's face reddened and she looked away. "Do I?"

"Finn Langley. He came home recently with lip stain on his cheek." It probably wasn't a good idea to make an enemy of the person taking care of her but she couldn't help it.

Audra turned back around. Her blush had faded and she smiled. "You got yourself a good one. Nearly had me sprawled on the dirty saloon floor when I sat on his lap. He told me he was married. Most of the time it doesn't matter to the men at the saloon, but he was not happy with the attention I gave him." Her smile widened. "Hold on to that one."

Maureen swallowed hard. Would it be possible to hold on to him now? She doubted it. Finn was here to make his fortune, not to rescue a criminal. He was on the run himself but he had told her about it. He'd been honest. Could he forgive her? Did he even want to?

Audra had a plate of fried chicken in the basket. She handed it to Maureen and gave her a sad smile. "If you end up with nowhere to go, come see me at the saloon."

Maureen nodded and swallowed hard. "Thank you," she croaked. She hadn't thought that far ahead. Her future was going back to Missouri with Mr. Jones. She watched as Audra put her cloak back on and left.

After setting the plate down at one end of the bed, she sat on the other end. Why hadn't she become a wife in truth? At least Finn would have been gentle. Carlton wasn't a gentle man, and he liked to hurt her. There were so many miles they'd have to travel. That probably had been his plan. He'd always tried to get her alone, but his wife had a knack for always being around.

She'd been free for a while and it'd been heaven. Could she live the next four and a half years on the memories of the last few months? She stood and began to pace. She'd eventually forget Finn's face and voice. It would all fade away, and she had no one to blame but herself. He'd forget her too. The need to apologize to him overwhelmed her. Would he even come before Carlton took her away?

She patted the place over her heart where she pinned the Irish lace Finn had given her. He'd need to have it back to give to his next wife. He'd probably have many children to help run the ranch. By the time she finished her contract, she'd be an old maid, and her choices for a good match would be extremely limited. Oh, what difference did it make? No one would ever come close to comparing to Finn.

The door opened again and it was Carlton. Thank goodness there were bars between them. He had his walking stick with him; it was just for show. He rummaged through the sheriff's desk and pulled out a key ring. The smirk on his face as he jangled them in front of her sickened her.

He came to the cell door, and she plastered herself to the back wall of the cell in fear. The click of the lock opening frightened her beyond reason. She knew better than to cry out. It would only make things worse.

He walked into the cell, his face twisted in a leer, and then he yanked her from the wall and walked her over to the bars. "Hold on to the bars while you get what's coming to you."

Her knuckles where white as she stood straight and tall. The first strike with the walking stick took her breath away. He'd never hit her that hard before. The second one almost brought her to her knees. He hit her from her shoulders to her thighs, over and over. She prayed for mercy and then she prayed that she'd pass out. Each blow hurt more than the one before, and finally she slid down to the ground. Any movement caused excruciating pain.

Carlton took the plate of food out of the cell and then he placed the sheet on the bed. Next, he yanked her up onto the bed and put a quilt over her.

"You tell anyone about this, and you'll get worse tomorrow. Understand?"

She could barely nod so he grabbed the back of her hair. "What?"

"I-I understand."

He dropped her head down and she closed her eyes and stayed absolutely still until the cell was once again locked. He slammed the door behind him when he left.

Tears poured out of her eyes but it hurt too much to sob. To think she'd been so mad at Finn when he'd spanked her. That was nothing. It had better take a while for the legal information to get to the sheriff. She wouldn't be able to sit a horse anytime soon.

She heard the door again and closed her eyes.

"It looks like you'll have to come back tomorrow, Finn. She's sleeping." The sheriff said as he approached the cell.

"Can't you just let me in there? She's my wife." Finn didn't sound mad. He sounded more sad than mad.

"Come back tomorrow, and you can spend all the time you want with her."

Finn sighed loudly. "I don't trust that Carlton Jones. Not one bit. I don't want him alone with her."

"Don't worry, I'm here and she's locked in. Go, get some sleep and we'll see you tomorrow."

There was silence for a bit then Finn answered. "You're right. I'll see you tomorrow."

The door opened and closed. Finally, she could breathe. Her heart broke. She'd have to give him up for good. Somehow, she'd have to make it so he wouldn't come after her. She felt dizzy and soon welcoming darkness washed over her.

CHAPTER EIGHT

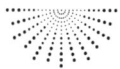

Finn spent most of the night constructing an "army" lockbox. He needed to have an empty one found on Maureen's side of the stream. He hoped that would put an end to people wanting her land. He'd had his valuables in a chest that looked close enough.

He scratched it up on the outside and dented it. He kicked it around the yard a bit. The hardest part was trying to figure out what to put in the box so it was certain to look like it was for the army. He thought on it for a while and then helped himself to Maureen's writing desk. He wrote a fake promotion for a nonexistent officer. No one would look at it too hard. He'd had a knack for forgery, so he signed it with flourishing handwriting. He waited until the ink was dry and then he folded it, rubbed dirt on it, crumpled it a bit, and then put a boot print on it.

Next chance he got he was going to bury it and try to lead his saloon friends, Cluck, Mesquite, and Bob to it. They'd have to be the ones to find it or they'd think he'd taken the money. The box could use a bit more if it was to be convincing. He'd get it all figured out.

The sun was coming up and he wanted to get at least an hour in reinforcing the roof before he went to town. He'd probably be there all day. He wanted nothing more than to knock Carlton's head off but then they'd have to run. If it came to it, he'd take Maureen and change their names and go elsewhere. He'd heard Canada wasn't half bad.

After he got his work done and he'd cleaned up, he saddled Justice. Justice didn't need much guidance; he knew the way to town. Finn pulled his hat down lower to keep the sun out of his eyes. He hadn't heard the option to become an indentured servant when he'd made his way over from Ireland. No one mentioned it while he lived in New York City. Strange but different states and territories differed.

They wouldn't want to leave for the east until winter was over. He'd heard stories of people getting lost in the snowy mountains. There was no way he'd allow his wife to leave alone with Carlton. Somehow, he'd accompany them and still get improvements on each section of land. But how? He only had four years before the land grant was revoked.

There was an uncommon silence in town. No people walked on the boardwalk. The absence of children playing in the street puzzled him. He dropped down off Justice and tied him to the hitching post. He walked into the Sheriff's office and he raised his brow. Maureen was the only one there.

"They left you here alone?" His voice was harsher than intended.

She gave him a wobbly smile and she seemed to have trouble standing up. "Only so they could go to the saloon and decide my fate. The sheriff demanded they wait until word came back with the law on indentured servants, but Carlton doesn't want to wait. He wants his property back."

"He plans to take you over the mountains at this time of year?"

Maureen nodded.

Finn walked to the cell took her hand and pulled her forward. He kissed her. "I'll be back, *a ghrá*."

His spurs clicked on the wooden walkway as he hurried to the saloon. He swung the doors open wide. He'd wanted to make an entrance and it worked. The place went quiet as everyone turned to stare at him.

"I hear you are determining the fate of my wife. It would have been nice if either her or I had been invited." He sat down in a chair in the front row. "Go on, I'd like to hear what you've decided so far."

Men exchanged guilty looks as the women looked down at the floor. Only Carlton met his gaze.

"As I was saying," Carlton said. "A man is entitled to his property."

"Not in this territory," Finn argued. "Furthermore, she is a white woman. A married woman. Doesn't a husband have a say over his wife? I would think a husband would have the right to refuse to let her go."

"Ha!" Carlton smiled. "She's a criminal first, my property second, and your wife third."

Finn stood and calmly faced the crowd. "I think you'll all agree that in the eyes of God she is my wife first. We were married by a minister. She told me why she ran away from you."

Finn smiled as Carlton turned a sickly white.

"I'm sure I don't know what you're talking about." Carlton suddenly didn't sound so pompous.

Finn looked at the sheriff. "How is he going to get her back to Missouri at this time of year?"

Carlton spoke first. "We plan to go back the way I came."

"I'm not sure you'll make it over those mountains. I heard the passes are closed. And I certainly don't want to go on a suicide trip."

Carlton took a step toward Finn. "This has nothing to do with you."

Finn laughed. "I go where my wife goes. Do you think I'm stupid enough to leave her alone with you? She left because you wouldn't stop touching her, and she was afraid you'd try to rape her."

The crowd gasped while Carlton turned a bright shade of red. The fury in his eyes appeared dangerous.

The sheriff put his hands up. "All right folks. I think we are done here. The mountain pass is closed, so they won't be traveling back anytime soon. By the time the pass is clear, I'll have confirmation on what the law is. Meanwhile, she will be released into the custody of her husband."

"I object!" Carlton yelled. "How do I know they won't run?"

The sheriff shook his head as though he'd had enough. "How much did you pay for her?"

"I paid the outrageous sum of twenty dollars for five years of work."

"I'll buy her from you!" a miner called out.

The sheriff held up his hand. "That's all for now folks. I'm going to have a private talk with Carlton and Finn in my office." He walked out the door obviously expecting both men to follow.

Twenty dollars was a lot of money. Finn could either pay for Maureen or have his ranch. He couldn't have both.

Maureen grimaced as she tried to sit up straight. She could feel her dress sticking to the broken skin on her back and shoulders. She needed a doctor, but who knew if prisoners were allowed doctors. Audra came in and brought her water to wash and a clean dress. Maureen thanked her but she hadn't been able to make use of either.

The door swung open and the sheriff, Carlton, and Finn all walked in. She wasn't sure if she should be relieved to see Finn or not. She kept her gaze on him, not knowing how much longer she had with him. She gloried in the sight of him and tried to commit his face to memory.

"Just where am I supposed to spend the winter if we don't leave now?" Carlton took off his gloves and slapped then against the desk.

The sheriff sat at his desk and balanced his chair on the back two legs. "You could claim some land of your own. I'd advise getting a cabin built quickly. The nights are getting cold. Or you can keep staying at the saloon. Makes no never mind to me."

Maureen watched the interaction. What in tarnation was going on? She glanced at Finn who smiled at her.

"I'm taking my wife home, today."

"Oh no, you're not!" Carlton ground out. He glared at her.

"Well, I have an idea." The sheriff shook his head. "Well, not an idea really. This is how it's going to go. Finn you come up with twenty dollars for me to hold. It'll be assurance you won't run. Maureen you can go home with your husband for now. Don't anyone get too comfortable. I'm still waiting to hear from the Territorial Governor. It'll take a while for my request to make it up the chain of command to his desk, I'm afraid." He stood, grabbed his keys, and opened the cell door. "You're free to go."

She tried to stand but the pain was too great and she cried out.

"Darling what's wrong?" Finn fled into the cell and knelt before her.

"Carlton punished me for running away. I don't think I can walk more than a few steps." Tears filled her eyes.

Finn unbuttoned the front of her dress and then pulled it down in the back. "Oh, my dear Lord. You must be suffering something awful." Finn glared at Carlton.

"Sheriff, would you mind coming in here?"

The sheriff wrinkled his brow but did as asked. There was a sharp intake of breath when he looked at the welts and broken skin on her back. He walked out, opened the other cell door, and shoved Carlton into it slamming the door behind him.

"I'll fetch Doc Adams." He hurried out the door.

"What kind of animal are you?" Finn yelled.

"It would have not been as severe but she married without permission and gave you her virginity. That was mine to take." Carlton sneered.

"Finn, don't waste your time on him. He's a bad seed. I knew it the moment I saw him, and I prayed and prayed that he'd buy someone else, but I ended up with him. He's not right in the head, I think. He really thought we'd make it through the mountain pass, just me and him. I'm in no condition to walk or ride now."

Finn helped to lay her on her stomach and then hung a sheet between the cells, giving them privacy. He sat down on a bit of the bed and stroked her hair. "Don't you worry, love. I'm pressing charges. He'll be in here until a territorial judge comes out this way. It's a small town so I doubt it will be high on his list of places to stop." He kissed the top of her head. It was one of the only places she wasn't injured.

"He used his walking cane on me. It hurts so much, Finn." Her eyes filled with tears she swore she wouldn't shed.

The sheriff arrived with Doc Adams and another sheet was hung along the front of her cell for even more privacy. She wanted Finn with her, but the doctor thought it best if he stayed on the other side of the sheet. The doctor had to soak parts of her dress to get it unstuck from the blood on her back.

At first, she concentrated on keeping quiet but she just couldn't take it anymore. Her cries were loud, and she was sure they were disturbing to Finn. She heard Finn tell Carlton he was going to kill him more than once.

At last, the dress was off, and Doc Adams began to dress her wounds. The salve he used stung a bit but she clenched her hands into fists until her nails dug into her hands causing them to bleed. By the time he finished, she was exhausted. Her eyes kept closing but she wanting to know what was happening.

The doctor left, and she tried to hear what he was saying to Finn but they kept their voices too low. Once again, other people were making decisions for her. At least she'd have a more time with Finn before she had to leave. Was he was willing to part with twenty dollars? Twenty dollars was a fortune and Finn might not think she was worth it. If the governor sided with Carlton, he would lead them to their deaths and there didn't seem to be much she could do about it. She'd make sure Finn would know who to notify in Ireland, if they were even still there.

When she'd left for America she'd figured she'd most likely never see her family again, but to know it for a certainty broke her heart. Her throat went dry, and a deep loneliness washed over her. And for what? She'd never have any money to send home. She had failed them all.

Finn came into the cell and knelt down. His blue eyes were trying for reassurance, but he was unsuccessful. She loved him all the more for trying. For a moment, she wasn't sure what hurt more, her heart or her back. He'd never look at her with love again.

"The doc is going to give you some laudanum for the pain. It should make you sleep and then we will carry you to room at Bessie McGuire's Boarding House. It's clean there and you'll heal better. I'll be with you."

"No, Finn. You go finish your cabin. Build your ranch and make your fortune. There's nothing you can do for me. My fate is sealed. I know the Territorial Governor will side with Carlton and the judge probably would take Carlton's side. Beating women wasn't considered much of a crime to many men. Soon enough, I'll be trudging through the snow to Missouri. I'll never forget your kindness to me. I'll never forget you and what an amazing man you are. Before they get rid of the dress, please unpin the piece of Irish lace you gave me. Save it for another."

She watched his Adam's apple bob up and down before he nodded.

"Time to give you your medicine young lady," Doc Adam's said.

Finn stood and moved out of the way and her heart shattered. She took the laudanum and soon enough the world drifted away.

FINN CARRIED Maureen across the street and up a flight of stairs to their room. Mrs. McGuire went ahead of him, unlocked the door, and pulled back the bed covers for Finn to lay Maureen down.

"What a shame. Her skin is snowy white. I have a feeling she'll scar. Can I get you anything?"

Finn shook his head. "Thank you for letting us stay. It won't be too long. Our cabin is almost done."

She nodded. "Just the same I'll bring you a tray of food and coffee. You'll need water and a cloth in case she starts with fever."

"You've been too kind."

Mrs. McGuire smiled. "Not a problem. I'm happy to help. You look at your wife the same way Mr. McGuire looked at me. It's rare you know. Hold on to each other. I'm not sure how she became an indentured servant, but it's outlawed in many states, so don't give up hope."

Finn drew a chair up next to the bed. "That helps, thank you." He waited for her to leave before he stroked Maureen's hair. He took the covering off her back. The doctor said air would be good for it. He gasped when he saw the extent of her wounds. Leaning over he kissed her cheek. "I will never allow another to take a hand to you ever. You have my word. Oh Maureen, how I love you. My love for you is in every breath I take, every word I speak and in every thought I think."

"Should have known, I married an Irish poet," Maureen murmured.

"Wait until I sing to you," he teased. "Go back to sleep. You're safe."

She closed her eyes and her soft steady breathing let him know she was in painless slumber.

Even if she had told him the truth, there probably wasn't anything he could have done. She changed her name twice and who would have thought Carlton would come all this way for her? The man was crazy.

He sat with her through the night listening to the constant groans. Picturing himself choking Carlton didn't help much. He needed to get the cabin ready. It was just about done, and then he could take Maureen home. Carlton could rot in jail for all Finn cared. If Carlton won his case and was able to take Maureen this winter, well he'd die of some accident in the mountains and then Finn would bring Maureen back where she belonged. To the Langley Ranch.

It had been a week of traveling back and forth from the cabin to the boarding house, but to Finn it was worth it. The cabin was done, root cellar and all. He walked out of the sheriff's office. Still no word, but Maureen was allowed to go home. The sheriff didn't even ask for the twenty dollars.

Finn had a spring in his step as he strode down the wooden walk to the boarding house. He glanced at the saloon and saw Mesquite watching him. He'd have to bury the box soon. Mrs. McGuire's husband had been in the cavalry, and she gave him two mementos to put in the box to convince anyone looking that it was from the army. A button from her husband's uniform, and part of a folded letter with the broken wax seal from the army. Those things should be enough. He'd bury it after he got Maureen home, then find a way to have the bartender mention to Cluck that he'd seen something, but he wasn't sure what it might be… though it looked important.

Maureen smiled at him. She was sitting up in the bed.

"An improvement, I see," Finn said as he approached her. He leaned over and lightly brushed his lips over hers. Every time he saw her, he wanted her. He even chastised himself for being an unfeeling brute for wanting her while she was in pain. But he couldn't help it.

"I get to leave today, and guess what!" Her eyes were brighter than he'd seen in a long while.

"What?" Her smile was infectious.

"I get to go home with you for now. I can't wait to see the cabin," she enthused.

He stood up straight. "I hope it isn't too painful for you. I put every quilt onto the bottom of the wagon and I'm hoping it will be enough."

Maureen touched his arm and held on to it for a while before she spoke. "Let's not worry about it now. It's bound to be bumpy but it'll be worth it. Plus this place must be costing you a fortune."

He shrugged. "How well did you know the people you traveled the Oregon Trail with?"

Her brow furrowed. "The O'Brien's were good people. I didn't know them until the day before we left. They'd treated me with the utmost kindness and it was devastating when Mrs. O'Brien and the babe died. Why?"

"Did they have family?"

Maureen tilted her head and raised one brow. "No, it was one of Gail's biggest sorrows but they planned to have a big family of their own. Is there a reason you're asking me these questions?"

"I completely unloaded your wagon and there was some money in it. I thought if they had family I should send it to them."

"They sold everything and saved for a long time to go West. I never thought about the money."

She stared out the window for a minute then glanced back at him. "Is there enough to pay off my indenture papers?" she hesitantly asked.

"Yes, more than enough." He stared into her blue eyes and the love he saw humbled him. He was a lucky man indeed.

He broke off the stare. "This is the plan. I need to get you dressed, down the stairs and into the wagon. Unfortunately, I need you to be alert until then. I can give you laudanum for the ride but I can't carry you without damaging your healing wounds."

She bit her bottom lip. "I understand."

THE PAIN WAS BEYOND INTOLERABLE. First, she had to get to the edge of the bed. Finn put a huge gray dress on her and then her shoes. The dress was so big it didn't touch her back. Where on earth had he found such a thing? Then he helped her to slowly stand. She swallowed hard against the agony.

"One slow step at a time, *a ghrá*." He studied her face.

"I can do this. It hurts like the devil, but I'll make it through. I'll warn you though there will be tears and loud cries and as soon as we're out of town you might hear a few words you wouldn't expect to have ever heard from me." She took a step and cringed. "After that, I hope the laudanum kicks in."

Finn's lips twitched. "Where would a fair lass like you have learned such words?" They took another step.

"On a ship coming to America." She took a deep breath and took two steps.

"Well, sailors do have a way with words." He chuckled as they took two more steps.

Maureen stopped at the top of the stairs and gulped. "Give me a minute." She took a few deep breaths and asked God to help her.

Finn went down the first step and turned around. "Here hold onto my hands. Use my shoulders to help you step down."

"Too dang smart," she mumbled before she took the first step down. She started to sway but Finn righted her.

"What did you just say? I think it was about me." He stepped down and she slowly followed.

"I don't remember what I said. I think I'm addlebrained from all the pain." They went down another step.

"Then again it probably wasn't about me." They slowly stepped down. "After all you got lucky to have snagged a fellow like me."

Any other time she'd have enjoyed his banter but God love him. He was trying to keep her mind off her pain. "Lucky how?" Her voice was full of pain.

They stopped; she'd made it down the stairs. She stood very still and breathed deeply.

"Glad to see that Old Mrs. Potts' dress is doin' the trick," said Mrs. McGuire in a pleasant lilt as she held the front door open. "Sorry, I am, to have met you under such circumstances. Good luck to you, my dear."

Maureen gave her a quick smile. It was all she could summon. "Thank you."

Finn stood at her side and helped her onto the wooden walkway. "I'm very handsome, and my Irish brogue is intriguing."

If she could, she would have laughed. "Intriguing indeed, if you're not used to one."

Doctor Adams approached her and gave her the medicine with a drink of water.

"Let's wait a minute before we get you into the wagon I borrowed. My only hope is that Justice and Vala behave while pulling it."

She closed her eyes, trying to block out the crowd that had gathered. Most probably thought her a criminal. The laudanum worked fast. She swayed and Finn swung her up into his arms and handed her to someone in the wagon. She was assisted onto her stomach and then cocooned by more quilts than they owned. She closed her eyes and thankfully didn't remember the ride home.

CHAPTER NINE

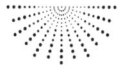

A week later, Finn peeked into the cabin and smiled. Maureen was sleeping and healing. She loved the cabin, and it made him feel ten feet tall. The way she tried to pretend she wasn't in pain was uncommonly brave and he found himself admiring her more each day. She tried to get out of bed and do some work around the cabin every day, and when he caught her, he'd gently lead her back to bed.

The loving looks they exchanged we're a highlight for him.

He closed the door and went back to his covered wagon. The box he'd fashioned was there, and he took a lock off one of his trunks. He needed to make it look old. Using his saw, he scratched it up, and then for good measure, he dented it with a hammer a few times. Then he rolled it in mud and let it dry.

Next, he wrote a note using Maureen's paper and ink, taking care to make the writing look different from the forged letter promoting the army officer that he'd written a couple of weeks earlier. He vaguely described a plan and gave the name of a location many miles away. Hopefully, it would look as though one of the gang went back for the money and left a note letting the others know where to meet him. He spilled coffee on the edges of the note and crumpled it a bit.

Finally, he set the note, button, and wax-sealed paper and the promotion letter in the box and put the broken lock on it. He then placed it in a bag and tied that to his saddle. He swung up on Justice, pulled his coat collar up against the chill, and rode off.

The tingling in the back of his neck let him know someone was trailing him. Maybe leading someone to the "treasure" would be easier than he'd first thought. But for now, hopefully he'd bore his follower with his meandering and whoever it was would leave. First, Finn rode the property line of Maureen's land. It was good land with rich soil, plenty of grass and water. He got down off Justice many times examining the soil and looking at watering holes.

At one point, he just sat in the grass and looked at the clouds. He picked up rocks looking at them and eventually the tingling was gone. He went into a wooded area and waited for a bit to be sure he was right. There was no sign of anyone trailing him.

Still, he waited a bit longer, dreaming of the cattle and horses he'd one day have. He also needed some type of landmark to make it easier for a person to locate the box. He decided on a spot between a big boulder and a tree. He swung down, grabbed his shovel, and buried the box. Then he walked over the filled-in hole and had Justice do the same. He tore down a few dead limbs off the tree and placed them on top.

He put the shovel away and rode off. Tomorrow he'd lead whoever was dogging him to the box. That should put an end to the tall tale of treasure.

Pleased, he rode home but a frown replaced his grin when

the cabin came into sight. Carlton's horse was tied outside. Anger and fear for Maureen filled him as he grabbed his rifle and walked to the door.

He wasn't surprised to find the door locked.

"Don't try coming in," Carlton yelled. "I'm going to get what's mine. I'll be out when I'm finished."

What was he talking about? Then it hit him: The man planned to bed Maureen. Well, that wasn't going to happen.

"Let's talk about this. Maureen is my wife, and she's injured!"

There was no answer. He slipped around the back of the cabin and walked a bit downhill until he came to the tunnel he'd built. He moved the branches hiding the entrance, and in he went. He stopped under the house. He'd made an obvious door in the floor for the root cellar but he'd made the getaway door less obvious. He'd learned from his years in Ireland to always have an escape plan.

He stood and listened. So far, Carlton was listing every mistake Maureen had ever made, including making him fall in love with her.

Finn waited. When Carlton went to the bed, Finn could come up behind him. But Carlton was in no hurry. He sat down and drank coffee. How stupid was this Carlton? Finn could have gone to get the sheriff. Why wasn't he in a hurry?

Suddenly, the heavy scraping sound of the chair legs pushed adrenalin through Finn. He waited until he heard Carlton's footsteps stop by the bed. Finn silently pushed up on the entrance and trained his rifle on Carlton.

"Kindly take a step away from my wife." His voice was hard as stone.

Carlton turned in surprise and fumbled, trying to get out his gun. Finn shot him in the arm. It was the farthest body part away from Maureen. Howling, Carlton hit the floor with a big thud, and Finn took the firearm away.

"Are you all right, *a ghrá*?" he asked without taking his gaze off Carlton.

"I'm fine. He's bleeding pretty bad. Maybe you should give him a towel or something."

Carlton gave her a nasty look. "I need a doctor, you nitwit."

Finn was going to punch Carlton in the face for his remark, but horses could be heard galloping up to the cabin. Finn walked backward keeping his rifle trained on Carlton the whole time and then reached behind him and opened the door.

The sheriff and a few of the other townsmen came busting in with guns waving. Shaking his head, the sheriff put his gun in his holster and advanced on Carlton. He grabbed Carlton's good arm and dragged him toward the door.

"Sorry about this. He clobbered me from behind when I let him out to use the privy," the sheriff said. "You're free and clear Maureen. There are no indentures in Missouri. Not any legal ones, at least." He pulled Carlton none too gently out the door.

Tears streamed down Maureen's face. Concerned, Finn sat on the bed and stroked her lovely red hair. "Are you hurting?"

She shook her head. "No, for once these are tears of joy. I'm no longer a fugitive. I get to stay here with you and build a life. That is, if you still want me. You have the right to change your mind. I've brought so much trouble into your life and—"

He leaned down and softly pressed his lips against hers. Her moan of pleasure emboldened him to deepen the kiss. She tasted like coffee and mint. She pushed her silky lips against his and wrapped her arms around his neck. Her fingers running through his hair was driving him insane.

Slowly, he broke the kiss and pressed his forehead against hers.

It took a moment for his breathing to even out. "I never want you to leave. You've become a part of me. I'm not exactly sure how it all happened, but I don't want to be without you. As I rode out there today, I pictured cattle and horses across our land. In my mind's eye, I can see a prosperous ranch. I have no doubt that we can build it together."

The big smile she gave him warmed him down to his toes. "I feel as though I can finally breathe. There will be no more looking over my shoulder. I should have told you the whole of it, but I didn't know how. I planned to a million times but I always lost my nerve like a fearful chicken."

"Speaking of chickens, I'm hoping to lead Cluck and his friends to the army box tomorrow."

Her expression became serious. "You best be careful. The box looked authentic to me, but there could be trouble. They might just shoot you out of your saddle as soon as they see the box."

He stood and kissed her forehead. "You rest and get better. I still haven't had my wedding night." She turned a lovely shade of pink but she didn't shy away.

THE NEXT MORNING Finn headed out again, this time leading his follower to the area where the box was. Finn got down off Justice and got his shovel and purposely dug in places near the box. Soon enough, Cluck, Mesquite, and Bob rode up.

"Hey, fellas! Maybe you can give me a hand. I got a tip about a box being buried in this area. Not sure what's in it, but if it's valuable, we can split it four ways." The hardest part was playing dumb enough to be convincing, but he needn't have worried.

The greedy eedjits eagerly climbed off their mounts, ready to dig for the treasure. Finn let them have at it for a bit before he subtly edged over to the place where the box was buried.

He dug and hit metal. They all turned toward the sound and excitedly swarmed around Finn.

"Here give me the shovel," Bob demanded, yanking it from Finn's unresisting fingers.

Finn scratched his chin. "Do you think it's the box of gold? I could use a bit of cash to get this ranch going."

Bob kept digging, and when they saw the box was black they grew even more excited. Bob took the box out of the ground and held it close to him. Then he frowned. "A bit light for gold."

"Maybe there's a treasure map," Mesquite suggested excitedly.

"Well, open it," Cluck said.

Bob put it on the ground and examined the broken lock. His tongue poked out and he licked his lips then opened the box. He stared inside, his brow furrowed. He handed the note to Mesquite who handed it to Cluck who handed it to Finn.

"Cain't read," muttered the former chicken farmer.

"Meet me in Dodge City. You know the spot. I'll be there to give you your cut," Finn read aloud.

"Let me see that!" Bob demanded. He looked at the paper and turned it this way and that. "How long do you think this has been here?"

"It looks really old," Mesquite said bitterly. "I was counting on that money."

"It could look old because it's been in the ground. I'm sure it wasn't written here. Maybe it got all crumpled on the way here. Either way, don't you think it's worth checking out?" suggested Finn. "Heck, if I didn't have to nurse my ailing wife, I'd jump at a chance and go." Finn sighed loudly.

"If we go, we get your share," Bob said, giving Finn a cold look.

"Now, hold on a minute. This was found on my land. I should get something," Finn said.

Cluck crossed his arms. "Makes sense that the people going to Dodge City should get the money."

Finn sighed. "I still don't think it's right but it's three to one. I lose out. Part of me understands but part of me was dreaming about what I could do if I had any money. You won't change your mind?"

"Don't get any ideas," Bob warned. "You don't want your pretty wife to be a widow, do you?"

"Tough break," Mesquite said, though his grin told another tale.

Finn kicked the ground. "I wish you the best of luck. If I wasn't married, I'd go along but I can't. If you ever come this way again, you can buy me a drink." He sighed and climbed into the saddle. "I'd best go and tend my wife."

"Say, you aren't going to come after us are you?" Bob asked.

"No, I'll be busy protecting what's mine and planting more explosives. Most times in life someone wins and someone loses. Think of the story you'll have to tell when you get the gold. God speed." He turned Justice and kept his horse to a slow trot. Finn would have rather full out run, but he didn't want them suspicious. They were greedy enough not to show anyone else the evidence. He rode to a place where he had the advantage and watched them ride off toward the East.

Grinning, he shook his head. He hoped they had enough sense to hole up for the winter. They'd be long dead before spring if they didn't. He shrugged. That was not his problem.

He took a deep breath. They were free. Finn quickly reburied the box in case he needed it again.

He gloried in the sun, the wind, the trees swaying and the green grass. He hoped there weren't any other secrets. He liked this feeling of the weight of the world off his shoulders. It was a first since he had come to America.

MAUREEN GOT up and dressed herself. She couldn't concentrate, so she paced. What was Finn thinking by tricking those men? She'd always thought him a smart man, but now she wasn't sure. He'd better come back to her. They hadn't even had a chance to have a normal life together. Her imagination wouldn't slow. She kept picturing all sorts of horrible things happening to him.

At least she knew where the secret escape door was. The man was crafty, though he could be a bit of a puzzle at times. They wouldn't have to worry about Indian attacks. They could run through the tunnel. The more she thought about it the more she realized he must have been an important man for the cause of Ireland. Why else put a price on his head?

It was rarely done. He was a hero, trying to break the bonds shackling the people by the British. In many ways, it was just like the way he helped to free her. Would they ever see a free Ireland in their lifetime? She'd never understood how those in power could just let people be burned out of their houses and left to starve. Who was going to do all the work for all the Lords of the Manors? But it was as though they didn't care how many died. The fact that both she and Finn knew how to read and write was a novelty. It was forbidden to them, as was speaking their Gaelic language. Their religion had been taken from them. They were no longer allowed to be Catholics but were made to attend protestant churches. They couldn't own land, or a horse worth more than five pounds. What was never counted on was the stubbornness and conviction of the strong people of Ireland. Yet, even though they'd become a nation of paupers, they'd found a way. They kept many of their traditions alive and they'd handed down their stories.

It was hard to watch every able-bodied person work so hard and earn so little. She swore people aged too early and died too young. But when she'd gotten off the ship, she realized to her dismay that she'd traded one type of bondage for another. Now to find out it had all been illegal, she wanted to be sick. She was so stupid to believe the captain who'd sold her. She could have found work and sent money home.

Why did others take advantage when they could? Was there really so much evil in the world? And what had become of her family? Were any of them still alive?

She and Finn would have strong children who knew what it meant to be free. They already owned land. She'd tell them the stories of hardship and bondage of the Irish people. She'd teach them to speak Gaelic. They'd practice their own Catholic religion. God willing they would all thrive and she'd be sure they were educated.

She took her shoes and stockings off and walked outside. The ground was cold, but she dug her toes into the earth. She owned this land. Imagine a woman owning anything. God had been looking out for her. It was strange, but she felt connected to the land.

She spied Finn riding in and waved.

He swung down and stared at her feet with his brow furrowed.

"Finn Langley, we are land owners. We are free and we own land. It's an amazing thing." She smiled.

"I felt the same way when I went into the land office. I was waiting for them to say you're Irish, you can't have land, but this is America. My whole being filled with pride when I signed the paper. I didn't have to sign by making an X! I signed my name."

She laughed when Finn swung her up into his arms.

"You, my dear, are supposed to be inside." He held her close as he stepped across the threshold.

"I'm tired of resting."

He set her down in the rocking chair he'd made for her and filled a basin with warm water. Then he took a cloth and knelt in front of her. He wet the cloth and washed her feet for her. Such a simple act but it made her love him all the more.

"You've taken such good care of me, Finn, and I thank you."

"Who was going to do all the cooking and cleaning if something happened to you?" He laughed. "It's been a pleasure. I know you'd do the same for me."

"Yes I would." Happiness flooded her being, and she prayed it never left. "It's been nonstop action since you parked your wagon across from mine."

Finn's laugh started as a low rumble in his chest and then he burst into hearty guffaws that went on for a good length of time. "I spent the first of it trying to catch a glimpse of your husband. One thing I can say is that you are never boring, Maureen."

She chuckled softly. "I had to steal clothes that fit a very big man to put on the clothes line. I wanted you to be wary of him."

"You did go to great lengths."

She grew silent for a moment. "You know what it's like to run for your freedom. I was willing to try anything to keep from going back. But my antics led me to you, so it worked out well."

His eyes filled with love and her whole body shivered. "It

did work out well. I thought myself a fool for not changing my name, but my name is all I came into the world with. The Langley's stood for honesty, integrity, and being loyal to Ireland. I believe in Beare and Forebeare as my ancestors did. I wasn't about to allow the English to take that from me too. There will be some lads following next year to expand the American Fenian Brotherhood."

"That won't be dangerous will it?"

Finn smiled. "Someday I'll tell you stories that will curl your hair."

"Finn, what did you do in Ireland?"

"I was a recruiter and a gun runner." He drew a breath. "And I was part of a small group that set charges and blew up strategic targets." One shoulder lifted in a haphazard shrug. "Like I said, I have stories that will take your breath away. I was a captain and I knew sooner or later they'd hang me or put me against the bloody wall where so many of my mates were executed so I escaped and came to America. I'll never stop trying to contribute in any way I can. The cause was my whole life."

"You miss it."

"Aye, I do, but fate has led me to a different life with you. You've become more to me than I ever thought a woman could. I was always willing to die, but now I have the greatest reason to stay alive, you."

He carried her to bed and kissed her lips, then her neck, and her shoulder... He began to pull away but she took hold of his hand.

"When will you make me a wife, Finn?"

"As soon as you're healed, *a ghrá*. It'll be soon. Right now, I have to be sure all the chores are done. Once I'm in your bed you, won't want me to leave." He gave her one of his sexy grins.

"Full of yourself aren't you?" she teased, but butterflies stirred in her stomach and her heart thumped erratically.

He stood and winked. "You wait and see. I have more wood to chop."

She shook her head as he closed the door behind him. Conceited was what he was. She lay back on her pillow, and suddenly she was filled with a wanting so strong she'd never known anything like it. Someday had better be soon.

CHAPTER TEN

*W*as she ready or not? The question swirled in his head all day. He'd spent the last week being very productive. He'd hunted, built the rest of the barn, and chopped a ton of wood. He was certain they had enough food for the winter.

Maureen, God love her, kept giving him sultry looks, and she probably had no idea what she was doing. Now that the time had come, he was as nervous as a schoolboy. She wanted him; it showed in each kiss she gave him. Did she know it would hurt the first time? Probably not. It wouldn't be something her mother would have talked about.

The first snowflakes began floating from the sky, and he smiled. He went into the house and told Maureen to get her wrap. When he led her outside, she smiled.

"I've never seen snowflakes so big before. If this keeps up we'll be buried in snow."

"I think we'll find plenty to do if that happens." His voice was husky.

Her face turned crimson and not from the cold. "Perhaps."

"How's your back healing?"

She gazed at him and shook her head. "Seeing as you tend to it each evening, you'd know better than I."

"Has anyone ever talked to you about the first time you're with a man?" His voice was so gentle and caring.

Her eyes widened and she shook her head.

Finn took her hand. "It hurts the first time. You're maidenhood needs to be breached. But only the first time. After that it should be pleasant."

"Are you saying you want to… now?"

"We can wait if you want. We've waited this long."

She put her arms around his waist and held him tight. "I've been waiting for this day, but I confess I'm nervous. What if I do something wrong? What if I'm not what you expected?"

He put his arms around her and rocked them both back and forth. "There is no wrong way. Don't worry." He took a step back and looked into her eyes. "Are you ready for this?"

She nodded. "Could you wait out here for a few minutes while I get ready?"

He smiled at her sudden shyness. "Of course I can honey. Take your time."

He paced while he bided his time. It would be fine, he kept telling himself. After an interminable wait, he went inside. Maureen was already in bed and her beautiful red hair fanned her pillow. He swallowed hard at the sight of her.

For a few moments, he stood in front of the roaring fire, warming his hands. Then he approached the bed. He began to get undressed, expecting her to turn away, but she didn't. What if she didn't like the way he looked? He should have insisted they wait until dark.

As quick as he could, he slipped under the covers. They lay side by side, staring at the ceiling. Finn laughed. "Let's look at each other instead."

They turned toward each other, and the love he saw reflected in her eyes erased all doubts. He reached for her and kissed her like there was no tomorrow. She kissed him back the same way. A shiver raced through her.

"Are you cold?"

She shook her head. "No, I guess my body is reacting to yours."

That was all the encouragement he needed. He stroked her and kissed her until she was ready. She cried out in pain for a second, and he paused, but then she released a sigh and smiled, and he began to love her again, not stopping until both their bodies shook with pleasure.

He rolled onto his back and pulled her with him so her head was on his chest. "Are you all right?"

She nodded.

Why didn't she say something?

"Maureen, did I hurt you?"

"It only hurt for a minute. The rest brought me a joy I never imagined before. I always thought it was a woman's duty. I never heard anyone mention joy. Joy doesn't even capture the feeling. It is much more than that." She snuggled against him and yawned. "Tell me again why we waited so long?"

Finn began to laugh, but before he could answer, Maureen had fallen asleep. He tucked her hair behind her ear and basked in his happiness. It was nice to have confirmation of what he'd thought all along: they'd be good together. Well, maybe not *all* along.

MAUREEN SNUGGLED CLOSER TO FINN, and her eyes quickly opened. They were both naked. She'd never slept without her nightgown on. Her hand was on his chest and the springy hair on it intrigued her. He was well muscled. She touched his shoulders and his hard stomach. Finn coughed, and she abruptly stopped.

"I didn't mean to wake you. There's at least an hour before we get up."

He pulled her close and whispered in her ear, "I know something we can do for an hour."

"But it's morning!"

"There aren't any hard and fast rules about when we make love. Come here."

She eagerly kissed him.

Afterward, she put her dress on while she was still under the sheets. She stood and Finn's lips twitched as though he was trying not to laugh. "What's so funny?"

"Your modesty, I suppose. Actually, I don't know what I was laughing about. Modesty is a good thing."

She went to the cook stove, and when she heard Finn behind her, she put her hands on her hips. "I think you'd better go and bring in some more wood." Then she ignored him and started breakfast.

"Yes, you're sassy all right. I like sassy." The door closed behind him.

Maureen laughed. It was a bit awkward, but they'd be spending their lives together so they'd best get used to it.

She cooked the bacon and made pancakes. She was just pouring the coffee when he walked in with an armful wood.

Finn stacked the wood near the stove and then stood behind Maureen, wrapping his arms around her. She giggled when he kissed her behind her neck.

"You've made me a happy man."

She turned her head to try to look at him. "Really? I mean it made me happy but I wasn't sure about…"

He tightened his hold on her. "You were perfect."

At a loss for words, she motioned toward the table.

"Breakfast."

He let go of her and sat down. "Looks good."

"Finn, when do you think we'll have a tiny bit of extra money?" She pushed her food around her plate.

He shrugged. "We have enough you don't need to worry about us."

"Well, what I mean is do you think we'll have enough to send back home after next year? I know you plan to harvest hay, and I was just wondering." She couldn't look at him. He was working so hard all the time, she shouldn't have asked.

"I've sent out a few letters to my contacts in County Mayo in the hope that they knew where your family had settled. As soon as we find them, we can send some money."

Maureen tilted her head and studied him. "Thank you for trying to find them. I don't want to send it unless we can spare it."

Finn put his fork down and reached across the table, covering her hand with his. "I was well cared for. My friends got me on a ship and gave me enough funds to start a new life. I've been pretty frugal. It'll be fine. Plus we still have some of the money I found in your wagon."

She nodded and smiled. "I really thought I'd be able to send money to my family sooner. But last I heard they've avoided the workhouses."

Finn got up and added more wood to the fire. "That's for the best. Once you go in, you don't come out no matter how young you are when you go in. They work you until there's nothing left of you. Most people know to avoid them. I'll go check on the horses and your mule."

How incredible it was to feel completely at ease with Finn. Her nerves had been working overtime in anticipation of their wedding night. There had been so many stories and opinions told, while she was in steerage coming over to America, she wasn't sure what was true. The younger women told her it was just fine while the older ones bemoaned about the duty they had to do each night. Frankly, it had scared her.

It was a fine thing not to have to worry about such things anymore. They had a wonderful time together. The door opened and she could see the snow coming down heavily. Finn stomped inside, his face red with cold.

"I suppose this is just the beginning of the bad weather," she said. "Come sit by—"

"Your horse is gone," he blurted. "I'm going to take Justice and see if I can find Vala. Let's hope that horse is smarter than she looks."

"I know you're annoyed, but she's a smart horse."

Finn got his bedroll together. "You're right. I'd rather snuggle with my wife than chase a horse in the falling snow. I tied a rope from the house to the barn in case I'm not back. I left Contrary plenty of food, but you never know. If for any reason you do need to go out to the barn, be sure to hold on tight to the rope. People have died not ten feet away from their homes because the snow and wind made it impossible to see. Keep a lantern burning in the window for me too."

She helped Finn gather supplies and then she hugged him close, wishing she didn't have to let him go. "Don't get lost out there. She'll probably come back on her own."

He gave her a long lingering kiss before he walked out the door. The wind was wickedly fierce, and the cabin was instantly chilled. Maureen added more wood to the fire and began to worry. She tried to keep busy sewing herself a warmer dress, but she kept opening the door to check for Finn. Soon she began to pace, and when he missed the noon meal, her stomach began to feel as though it was tied in knots.

After taking a few deep breaths, she went back to sewing her wool dress. It was a pretty shade of blue that Finn said matched her eyes. It didn't take long before she pricked her finger with the needle. She set it aside again. It wouldn't do to get blood on the fabric.

Darkness was beginning to descend, and she lit the oil lamp. The problem was, where to put it. They didn't have glass for their windows. They just had shutters. She pushed the table to the window and set the lamp on it. Then she opened the shutters just enough to let the light out. Did they have enough oil left? They'd been using candles since they were cheaper. After wrapping two blankets around her shoulders, she sat in her rocking chair by the wood burning stove.

Where was he? Was he safe? Then she heard a wolf howl and the answering howls of other wolves answering. Closing her eyes, she prayed for Finn's safety. It was all in God's hands now.

The shutter opened inward a bit.

"Dang wind." She rose to secure the shutter and was met by the glowing eyes of a wolf. Her scream echoed off the cabin walls, but it remained undeterred. In fact it looked about to jump into the cabin. Gritting her teeth, she raced over to slam and lock the shutter. The wolf scratched at the shutters with its long claws. The sound sent shivers down her spine.

She grabbed the rifle they had hung on the wall and made sure it was loaded. She grabbed extra shells and put them in her apron pocket. She widened her eyes as she heard a sound on the roof. Sure enough, a wolf was walking up there. The click, click, click of its feet made her skin crawl. How in the world did it get up there? Why wouldn't they just leave? Then another scratched relentlessly at the door. She didn't know which way to turn.

The moon was full and she could suddenly see a sliver of silver light shining in from a hole a wolf had made by digging at the mud and grass chinking they'd put between the logs.

From the hole, she could see that there were at least four of the dangerous beasts out there.

The one on the roof was now hitting the stove chimney. Ashes poured down onto the fire, sending black soot everywhere. She grabbed more wood and added it to the fire. She hoped Finn was hunkered down somewhere safe. The wolves were frightening, but she'd be able to keep them out.

She put coffee on; it was going to be a long night. They weren't inviting more wolf friends with all their howling were they? The one at the window kept slamming against the shutter. Maureen quickly put the other two wood supports across to keep the shutter tight.

Why were they here? She'd only eaten bread and cheese for supper. She hadn't cooked any meat. Maybe they could smell her fear. A yawn overtook her, and she blinked her eyes, trying to wake up. No matter how much coffee she drank, she remained exhausted, but she didn't dare go to sleep. It was nerve-racking with the constant scratching, banging, and howling. At one point, she wanted to cover her ears and scream, but it wouldn't have helped, and she gritted her teeth instead.

Now she hoped Finn wasn't anywhere nearby. He'd be set upon by the wolves for sure if he tried to come home. He wouldn't be able to take on four wolves.

A gunshot exploded just outside, and she dove to the floor. Friend or foe? She peeked out the hole in the chinking and saw Justice's legs head toward the barn. Finn was home. How shored up was the barn? Did he need her to open the door and start shooting?

She wasn't that good of a shot. There was no way she'd hit a moving target. Another shot rang out, and a great big whimper followed. Then an eerie silence fell. Maureen put her ear to the door in case she needed to open it quickly for Finn, but she heard nothing.

It seemed like forever before she heard another shot. Scraping and scratching came from overhead, and the one on the roof fell to the ground, landing with a heavy thump. Thank goodness. That left only one maybe two left. She peeked out the hole again and saw the two wolves scamper off. Her body refused to relax. She needed to see Finn. She needed to touch him and know for certain he was fine.

FINN SPRINTED to the cabin and the door flung open. Maureen grabbed him, pulled him inside, and slammed the door shut.

He put his rifle down and took her into his arms. Her whole body was shaking as she held on tight. What a woman. He'd expected hysterics and tears, but instead she had every firearm ready to go.

He stroked her back. "We're all right. I'm so sorry I left you alone."

She let go and stared up at him. "Finn, it's part of pioneering in a new place. I was scared to death, and I was so worried about you. Did you know wolves are extremely strong? They call to one another by howling, and the next thing you know more come. They're sly too. One was on the roof shaking the chimney. Another kept trying to get in the window. Then another one started digging out the chinking. The worst was the one that kept slamming its body against the door." She finally took a breath. "What about Contrary? The poor mule."

"Contrary was huddled in the corner of her stall shaking but she's fine."

"They are known to be aggressive at times but this is the worst I've heard. I'm just glad you're safe."

"What about Vala?"

Finn shook his head. "I couldn't find a trace of her. I think she was stolen. She was in a stall. I just don't know what to think. It didn't occur to me until I was out in the drifts of snow that the barn door had been open." He cupped her cheeks in both hands and stared into her beautiful blue eyes. He kissed her for all he was worth then took a step back. "I have to get Justice settled."

Maureen nodded. Her eyes looked a bit dazed from his kiss. It made him glow inside and gave him warmth to carry within him while he was outside.

He brushed Justice down, put a blanket on him, and gave him extra feed. Contrary started pitching a fit. Finn laughed and gave her extra feed too. He'd planned to breed Vala, but now he'd have to change his plan.

Life was about learning to constantly adapt, it seemed. Holding on to the rope, he made his way back to the cabin. It was a good thing he'd arrived home when he did. The storm was worsening, and he could hardly see the house through the snowy wind. Relieved to finally get to the door, he opened it and stepped inside. Snow fell to the floor as he shrugged out of his outside gear and he happily took the cup of coffee Maureen offered.

"The storm looks awful, and the sound of it is worse."

He shook his head. "It certainly is. I'm glad I tied that rope from the barn to the house. I needed it to get back."

She grabbed a blanket she had warming near the fire and placed it on his shoulders. "I'll start some nice, hot stew for you."

He grabbed her hand and pulled her down into his lap. "How about you keep me warm instead?" Her rosy blush pleased him.

She buried her face in his chest. "You need to eat." She wasn't very insistent.

"How have you been feeling today?"

She glanced at him in askance. "Fine, I guess, except for the wolves."

"I mean are you sore?"

"Sore?"

He cleared his voice trying to figure out how to ask and still be delicate. "From last night and well, this morning too. Especially the first time, it can leave a woman sore."

Her face turned from a rosy red to a dark crimson. "I, um, well. I haven't noticed so I suppose I'm fine. What about you? Are you…sore?"

He turned his head away to keep from laughing, but he couldn't help it. He laughed long and hard. Maureen got up and folded her arms in front of her, watching him with one eyebrow raised, and he still couldn't stop. When she squared her shoulders, he clamped his mouth shut and forced himself to settle down.

"I'm sorry. I shouldn't have laughed at you." He stood and cupped her shoulders in his hands. "You're so innocent, and I love you for it. Men don't usually get sore. I guess I've never heard anyone ask that of a man before, and that's why I laughed."

She looked at the floor. "There are many things I don't know, Finn. Will you be laughing at me constantly?"

He tilted her head up with his finger. "No I won't. You are everything to me, and I feel so blessed to have found you. I love you with everything in me. I never knew love could be so strong."

Tears formed in her eyes. "I love you with my whole heart, Finn. We'll have a good life as long as we have each other."

Finn picked her up and put her on the bed.

"Finn!"

"*A ghrá*, I just want to show you just how much I love you."

EPILOGUE

From the grassy spot they'd picked for their picnic, Finn could see a good portion of their land. Cattle were grazing on the eastern portion while horses were frolicking in the western pasture. If he squinted, he could see the beginning of his hay growing in the field.

He'd hired a few men to help him out, and he was able to pay them and send money home to Maureen's family as soon as one of his most trusted friends had located them. He was one lucky Irishman to have found such a lass as Maureen. There was never a dull moment with her.

She was so much more than a wife and mother. She was his partner in all things. Not that she'd have it any other way, but she was smart and her input in decisions was always a help. Her horse Vala had found her way home about two weeks after he'd gone to find her. It was still a mystery where she'd been, but the only conclusion they came to was that someone knew the weather was going to be bad and had borrowed her.

Even up until the day she went into labor, Maureen

worked by his side. She refused to sit and relax. There'd never be another like her.

He laughed as she grabbed little Patrick and put him back on the blanket, only to have him crawl off it again. He was the very picture of her, red hair and all. It pleased him to have a son to carry on his legacy. The ranch was sustainable, and he imagined many children and grandchildren playing and working. *Beare and Forbeare*, the Langley motto was still lived by – be patient and endure. He could only hope that his legacy lived on and prospered. He took out his pocket watch and traced the shamrock with his finger. Maureen still wore the piece of Irish lace next to her heart and rejected the idea of a wedding ring. He planned to get her one anyway.

"Your turn, Daddy," Maureen said, out of breath.

Slipping his watch back into his pocket he then leaned over and gave Maureen a kiss on her sweet lips. Patrick gurgled his approval, as Finn scooped him up and settled him in his lap. Patrick stayed, staring at Finn the whole time. The look of wonder Patrick always had made Finn's heart swell with love and pride.

Maureen laughed. "How do you do that?"

"Do what?"

Maureen shook her head. "He'll sit still for you."

"*A ghrá*, he just likes me better is all." He gave Maureen one of the grins that usually left her speechless.

"You know, Maureen, ever since I was a lad I'd searched for my fortune. Finn's Fortune. Has a good ring to it, doesn't it? But when I had to escape to America, I thought I'd never have a fortune. I've learned many things over the years, but the most important one is fortune doesn't mean money. I have found my fortune in you and our son. Your love is worth all the money in the world to me. You make me want to be a better man. You brighten my days and the nights are heavenly. You my love are my fortune."

The End
I'm so pleased you chose to read Finn's Fortune, and it's my sincere hope that you enjoyed the story. I would appreciate if you'd consider posting a review. This can help an author tremendously in obtaining a readership. My many thanks. ~ Kathleen

AFTERWORD

Follow the Langley's rich family history through the years as told through the wonderful storytelling voices of these six bestselling authors.

1850 - Finn's Fortune - Kathleen Ball
Langley Legacy- 1850

Running from the British, captivating Finn Langley flees from Ireland to America with a price on his head. Finding treachery the handsome Irishman must travel further to hide. He joins a wagon train and heads for Oregon.

Maureen McDonald leaves Ireland and travels to America in the hope of sending much needed money back to her family. Upon arrival she had no other choice but to become an indentured servant. In trying to protect her virtue she realizes she must run away and ends up owning land in Oregon.

Both Finn and Maureen must fight to claim their land, their freedom, and each other. Will they get a chance to build both their amazing love and a lasting legacy- the Langley Legacy?

AFTERWORD

Beare and Forebeare
1875 - Patrick's Proposal - Hildie McQueen Amazon
Langley's Legacy - 1875
Patrick's Proposal

A rash marriage proposal changes their lives forever, but will it keep her from danger or make things worse?

Emma Davis has no recourse but to run for her life on a stormy night. Seeking shelter in a barn she prays for a reprieve from a life of misery. When the son of a family in good standing helps her, Emma knows he'll expect something in return. It's time to run again, but where can she possibly go?

Patrick Langley's life has been good but predictable. When a woman needing protection enters his life on a stormy night, little does he realize, just how much things are about to change. She brings equal parts of passion and danger. The first is stronger than any storm.

A story of trust and new beginnings.

" Beare and Forbeare"
1899 - Donovan's Deceit - Kathy Shaw Amazon
Langley Legacy-1899

Can love grow in a bed of lies?

After ten years of dodging the law, bounty hunters and Pinkerton agents, the infamous outlaw Donnie Langley wants to go straight. Only he'll have to "die" first.

AFTERWORD

In a bizarre twist of fate, Donovan finds his identical twin brother dead. The opportunity for Donovan to live his life as his law-abiding brother surrounded by family is too great to squander.

But his brother had secrets of his own. Like his impending marriage to the Sheriff's daughter.

Beare and Forebeare "Be patient and endure"

1933 - Aiden's Arrangement - Peggy McKenzie

Langley's Legacy - 1933

Can an arranged marriage between two feuding families create a new beginning and help them survive the catastrophic financial devastation of the Great Depression or will secrets and betrayal doom them all to failure?

Maura Jackson has heard about the feud between her family and the Langley's since she could walk. Her papa made certain she knew every despicable detail. She wanted to hate Aidan Langley. She needed to hate him. It was her duty to her family to hate him. But, ever since that hot summer day when she and Aidan caught each other swimming nude, she has had a hard time convincing herself what she feels for Aidan Langley is hate. It feels like so much more. Now, her parents have agreed to a business arrangement with the Langleys. She and Aidan will marry and have a child—the link that will bind the families together. But can she keep her part of this arrangement without losing her heart to the handsome enemy?

AFTERWORD

Aidan Langley's life had been pretty good up to this point. But when financial setbacks threaten to rob his family of everything his parents and the generations before them worked so hard to claim, he was agreeable to do just about anything—even when his parents asked him to marry Maura Jackson, the great niece of the man who accused his dad of ruining him and caused a black mark on his family's name. Could their union truly unite these two feuding families, or would their animosity toward each other tear them even farther apart? Aidan wasn't convinced it could work but he would do his duty to his family's legacy. One thing was for certain, his heart would never belong to Maura Jackson—and as soon as he lived up to his end of the bargain, he would set her free.

A story of perseverance and discovering love in the last place you expected to find it.

" Beare and Forbeare"

1968 - Heath's Homecoming - Merry Farmer Amazon
Langley Legacy - 1968

Returning Vietnam War vet Heath Langley has a powerful family legacy to live up to. But his experiences in the jungles of Vietnam, including losing his best friend, have left him struggling to find his place in the world. Everything he thought his life would be has changed, and he doesn't know how to keep up. Only one thing grounds him and keeps him going, the girl he left behind.

Barbie Rose is determined to be more than her mother's generation ever dreamed of being. She's well on her way after Aiden Langley hires her to manage Legacy Ranch. But not everyone likes seeing a woman in charge, and when Heath returns, her heart and her future hang in the balance.

AFTERWORD

Especially since she can see how much healing Heath has to do.

But what could be the perfect relationship hits a snag when Barbie and Heath find themselves at odds over the horse that their friend Davy left behind after giving the ultimate sacrifice for his country. Can they learn to compromise and find their way forward together, or will the Langley Legacy end with them?

Beare and Forebeare

Present - Collin's Challenge - Sylvia McDaniel Amazon

The Langley Legacy Present Day
    Can love overcome a generational feud?

For generations, Collin Langley's family has owned the largest Appaloosa ranch in New Dawn, Oregon. When a long lost member of the Jackson's lays claim to the land, reigniting the Langley-Jackson feud, he's more than irritated. When the judge allows her petition to live at the Legacy, he's furious. Except the red-haired beauty is not only gorgeous, but smart.

JoLeigh Jackson learns that the ascendant who joined the ancestral land with the Langley's wasn't the heir apparent. Needing a large piece of property to fulfill her dream of an animal genetics lab, JoLeigh files suit against the despised Langley's.

Can JoLeigh and Collin overcome secrets from the past? In the end, will possession of the land matter, or will love lay claim to their hearts.

AFTERWORD

"Beare and Forebeare" (be patient and endure)

ABOUT THE AUTHOR

Sexy Cowboys and the Women Who Love Them...
Finalist in the 2012 and 2015 RONE Awards.
Top Pick, Five Star Series from the Romance Review.
Kathleen Ball writes contemporary and historical western romance with great emotion and
memorable characters. Her books are award winners and have appeared on best sellers lists including: Amazon's Best Seller's List, All Romance Ebooks, Bookstrand, Desert Breeze Publishing and Secret Cravings Publishing Best Sellers list. She is the recipient of eight Editor's Choice Awards, and The Readers' Choice Award for Ryelee's Cowboy.
Winner of the Lear diamond award Best Historical Novel- Cinders' Bride
There's something about a cowboy

facebook.com/kathleenballwesternromance
twitter.com/kballauthor
instagram.com/author_kathleenball

OTHER BOOKS BY KATHLEEN

Lasso Spring Series

Callie's Heart

Lone Star Joy

Stetson's Storm

Dawson Ranch Series

Texas Haven

Ryelee's Cowboy

Cowboy Season Series

Summer's Desire

Autumn's Hope

Winter's Embrace

Spring's Delight

Mail Order Brides of Texas

Cinder's Bride

Keegan's Bride

Shane's Bride

Tramp's Bride

Poor Boy's Christmas

Oregon Trail Dreamin'

We've Only Just Begun

A Lifetime to Share

A Love Worth Searching For

So Many Roads to Choose

The Settlers

Greg

Juan

The Greatest Gift

Love So Deep

Luke's Fate

Whispered Love

Love Before Midnight

I'm Forever Yours

Finn's Fortune

Made in the USA
San Bernardino, CA
15 November 2018